MORE THAN FRIENDS

Ivy entered Ben's bedroom and found him struggling with the closure on a footlocker. She couldn't help but giggle at his predicament.

"Are you gonna help me, or just keep laughing? The lid won't close all the way."

"Hang on," Ivy said. "Let me sit on it, and then you can snap the lock in place."

Ben knelt in front of the trunk. He placed his hands on the lid and pressed his body weight onto it.

Ivy watched for a moment, then scooted onto the lid. Ben released his hold slowly, and then bent to the lock. He reached for a nearby padlock and slid it into place, brushing against Ivy's legs in the process. The unintentional contact sent tiny surges of electricity through them both. Ben raised up to a kneeling position, placing himself at eye level with Ivy.

"Thanks for your help," he said huskily. He started to move away, but Ivy stopped him with a warm hand on his cheek.

"I'm glad I could help," she replied, stroking her hand along his face.

"Ivy, don't," Ben pleaded.

"You don't want me to touch you?"

"I do want you to touch me, more than you can imagine, but you have insisted that you want us to be friends. And if you don't stop now, I can't promise I won't take this *friendship* to another level."

"What level is that?"

"Don't play with fire, Ivy."

Their eyes locked in an intimate stare, looking for permission to proceed or a warning to stop. Ivy finally broke the stalemate, sliding her hands to the back of his neck and guiding him gently past the last obstacle.

GOOD INTENTIONS

Crystal Wilson Harris

ARABESQUE
☆BET
BOOKS

BET Publications, LLC
www.bet.com
www.arabesquebooks.com

ARABESQUE BOOKS are published by

BET Publications, LLC
c/o BET BOOKS
One BET Plaza
1900 W Place NE
Washington, D.C. 20018-1211

All Kensington Titles, Imprints, and Distributed Lines are available at special quantity discounts for bulk purchases for sales promotion, premiums, fund-raising, and educational or institutional use.

Special book excerpts or customized printings can also be created to fit specific needs. For details, write or phone the office of the Kensington special sales manager: Kensington Publishing Corp., 850 Third Avenue, New York, NY 10022, attn: Special Sales Department. Phone: 1-800-221-2647.

First Printing: January, 2001

10 9 8 7 6 5 4 3 2 1
Printed in the United States of America

For Sharon and Julius, who have taught me it's much more important to be friends first

One

Sounds of retching and gagging filled the small lavatory, bouncing off the closed door, reverberating against the ceramic tiled walls. The woman crouched against the cool porcelain struggled valiantly to control the spasms, but her efforts met with limited success. The best she could hope for was keeping her lacy beaded veil out of the line of fire.

"Ivy? Honey, it's almost time." The disembodied voice from the other side of the door was muffled. "Are you OK?"

"Yes, ma'am. I'll be right there." Ivy Daniels spoke with a confidence she did not feel. She pushed away from the cool porcelain bowl and stumbled over to the sink. Snatching a handful of paper towels from the wall dispenser, Ivy wet them with cold water and patted her face, only moderately concerned about mussing her elaborate makeup. Ivy leaned on the sink, stared at the reflection in the mirror mounted above the sink, and tried to smile encouragingly.

"You're just a little nervous," she told the woman in the mirror, ignoring the hint of panic in her eyes. "All brides get the jitters. It's perfectly normal. Now you've got to go . . . there's a whole church full of people waiting for you out there."

Ivy reached for a dry paper towel and gingerly patted down her face. She carefully scrutinized her dark cocoa reflection. Her skin was flawlessly smooth and even-toned, making a color foundation unnecessary. Her bridesmaids had fussed over her face earlier, applying what Ivy felt was too much blush and too-thick eye shadow. Ivy had finally conceded to their ministrations, acknowledging that her friends were much more experienced with makeup. If they all said Ivy looked beautiful, that was good enough for her. Most of the makeup was where it was supposed to be, she noted with relief, except for her mascara. Black rings of the cosmetic circled her eyes, making them appear darker than they normally were.

Ivy muttered a curse and retrieved one of the wet paper towels from the wad on the edge of the sink. She wrapped her index finger in the moist paper and swiped under her eyes, trying to remove the excess mascara.

After a few moments of rubbing, Ivy threw the towel down in disgust. "I'll be wearing a veil," she muttered to her reflection. "Nobody's gonna see my eyes anyway." She reached up and fluffed out her veil, smoothing out the wrinkles from earlier. "Just take a deep breath," she ordered herself. "It'll all be over soon."

The knock at the door was more insistent this time. "Ivy? Honey, you've got to come on now . . . it's getting late."

Ivy spared one last glance at the mirror, consciously ignoring the sense of impending doom reflected in her eyes. She squared her shoulders and turned to unlock the lavatory door. She stepped out into the church's women's lounge, which for today's occasion had been transformed into a dressing room filled with frenzied activity.

"Ivy! Honey, I thought we were going to have to break this door down."

"You're being a little melodramatic, aren't you, Mom?" Ivy managed a smile at the older version of herself.

Grace Daniels shook her head emphatically. "I don't think so, young lady. We were all getting worried."

Ivy looked around the room at the faces of her wedding party. Her bridesmaids and maid of honor, four of her closest friends, all regarded her knowingly. Ivy knew what they were thinking. Having just partied together at the bachelorette bash until the wee hours of the morning, her friends undoubtedly thought Ivy was fighting the aftereffects of a hangover.

"What's wrong, Ivy?" asked Kim, her maid of honor. "Can't run with big dogs anymore?"

"She's turning into an old married lady already," one of the others chimed in. Ivy shook her head and smiled at the quartet of friends, all decked out in identical rose-colored chiffon.

"Don't you worry about me, Miss Kim. You need to make sure you can handle that walk down that aisle, 'cause as I recall, a few hours ago walking a straight line was the last thing you could do!"

The friends all burst into laughter. Grace Daniels shook her head in disapproval. "I don't want to hear any more," she said. "I don't even want to think about what you girls did last night."

"You're right, Mrs. Daniels," Kim agreed, "you really don't."

That comment sent gales of laughter through the room again. Grace turned away, but not before Ivy spied a smile on her mother's face.

"Ms. Williams here is ready to cue the organist." Grace gestured toward the wedding coordinator, who was readily identifiable by the clipboard in her hands, the spare pencils in her hair, and the sensible shoes on her feet.

"Yes, Ivy," Ms. Williams concurred. "A wedding should run like clockwork. Which means we need to start on time. Now are you ready?"

Ready is a relative term, Ivy thought. Forcing a smile onto her face, she reached for the elaborate bouquet of irises, white roses, and trailing English ivy her mother handed her. "Let's do this," Ivy said.

Ms. Williams nodded her approval and began shooing the bridesmaids out into the vestibule outside the main sanctuary. "Places, places everyone. It's time to begin."

Grace gave her daughter a reassuring hug. "It's going to be a beautiful wedding," Grace murmured into Ivy's ear.

"But what about the marriage?" The question slipped out of Ivy's mouth before she could rein it in. "Is it going to be a beautiful marriage?"

Grace pulled back and studied her daughter. "Of

course it is, honey. Keith is a great catch. He'll provide for you in high style for the rest of your life. You'll see."

I don't need to be provided for, Ivy's mind screamed. She wanted to protest but she held her tongue. Smiling weakly at her mother, Ivy returned the hug and then busied herself with fluffing the bouquet. Grace gave her one more supportive squeeze of the hand, and then hurried to the vestibule to line up for her grand entrance.

Ivy suddenly found herself alone in the lounge. In the silence, her thoughts and uncertainties could no longer be ignored. *God, I hope I'm doing the right thing.* She shook her head, viciously trying to scatter the uncomfortable thoughts. *Keith is a good catch,* she told herself. *He loves me, and we will be happy together.* In her mind's eye she saw the inside of the sanctuary filled to capacity with friends and relatives. "Besides," she said aloud, "what else can I do? It's too late."

A sharp rap on the door broke into her thoughts. "Come in," she called.

"Hi, baby. Ms. Williams sent me in here to get you. It's time for us to go."

"Hi, Daddy." Ivy's smile was genuine. "You look so handsome. Gray is your color."

Albert Daniels shrugged and grinned. "What can I say? I clean up well." He held his hand out to his daughter. "Ready for me to walk you down the aisle and give you away?"

"Daddy, do you believe in soul mates? That there is someone out there who is the person for you?"

"I don't know what you mean," Albert answered hesitantly.

"I mean, do you believe that everyone has a match in the universe?"

"Sure . . ." His voice was cautious.

"Do you think you'll know that person when he comes along?" Ivy asked.

"What's going on, baby? Something you want to talk about?" Albert studied his daughter carefully.

Ivy looked into the dark brown eyes of her daddy, her first true love. She felt unnamed emotions begin to swell in her throat. Finally she looked away. "No, sir. I guess I've just got prewedding nerves."

"You're sure?"

"Sure as I can be," Ivy mumbled. She reached for her father's hand and gave it a squeeze. "Come on, handsome. Let's go."

Albert looked at her carefully one more time. Then, apparently satisfied with what he saw, he held out his arm for her.

They left the lounge and emerged in the vestibule. The last of the bridesmaids was just entering the sanctuary. Ivy peeked through the double doors and got her first look at the decorated sanctuary. The room was long and deep. Approximately forty pews lined each side of the long center aisle. *Ms. Williams has outdone herself*, Ivy thought. Each pew was adorned with a small floral spray of ivy and baby's breath. Dozens of white tapered candles lit the front of the church. As Ivy watched, her rose-outfitted bridesmaids made the long walk to the front of the church each on the arm of a groomsman in a charcoal-gray tuxedo. Then she caught sight of her intended, standing patiently between the pastor and his best man, waiting for the ceremonies to begin. Ivy backed away from the door before anyone saw her peering in.

The sight of Keith stirred strong feelings in her. Unfortunately, they were not feelings of love. Instead, panic and dread bore down on her. *I don't love him,* she realized suddenly. *I'm about to walk down the aisle and commit my life to a man I don't truly love!*

The organ music changed as the maid of honor, Kim, reached the front of the church. The strains of the bridal march began to float from the sanctuary. The flower girl and her petal-dropping was all that remained before Ivy was escorted down the aisle by her father.

To Ivy, the organ music that swelled from inside the sanctuary seemed to close in on her with each pulsating note until she was literally gasping for air.

Sensing the distress in his daughter, Albert turned to look at her. "Ivy?" his voice trailed off in question.

"Daddy, I can't do this."

"Can't do what?"

Ivy gave him a look. "Daddy . . ."

Albert studied his only daughter closely. "Are you sure? All brides get nervous you know."

"It's more than nerves, Daddy. I am absolutely

sure. I have to go." She looked pleadingly into his eyes. "Tell them for me?"

Albert took a deep breath and sighed. "Where are you going to go?"

"I don't know for sure—just away from here." Ivy's brow wrinkled in frustration. "I didn't drive here—I don't have my car."

Albert patted his breast pocket. "I don't have my keys or my wallet. Grace put them in her purse so my jacket wouldn't bulge."

"Then I guess I'm hoofin' it." Ivy gathered her billowing skirts and lifted them a few inches so she wouldn't stumble.

"Wait a minute." Albert put a restraining hand on her arm. "Honey, you can't do this . . . not this way. Whatever else you think, Keith deserves an explanation. And from you—not me."

Ivy peeked inside the sanctuary again. The flower girl had almost reached the front of the church. "Daddy, I know you're right, but I can't right now. I have to get my thoughts together first. I promise I will talk to Keith later today."

Albert nodded and reached into his pants pocket. "Here's a couple of dollars. But I don't think it's enough for a cab."

The time-honored strains of "Here Comes the Bride" filled the church.

"It'll have to do." Ivy snatched the money from her father and bolted out of the church just as the ushers were opening the sanctuary doors for her grand walk down the aisle. Albert squared his shoulders, took a deep breath, and stepped into the sanctuary. The music trailed off as the organist realized the bride was not there. "Keith." Albert's voice filled the suddenly silent church. "I need to talk to you."

Two

"I'm on my way. I should be at your apartment within a half hour." Ben Stephens cradled the cordless phone between his ear and shoulder as he checked his wallet. "I've got the tickets right here."

The masculine voice on the other end of the line grumbled. "Tell me again why we're going so early? The game doesn't start for another two hours."

"Darryl, why do we go through this every game? You know I like to get to the stadium early to beat the crowds," Ben said patiently. "I like to watch the Cubs warm up."

"And you want to be on hand just in case any little old ladies need to be helped across the street, right?" Darryl Moore made a harumphing sound deep in his throat. "Man, you must have been a boy scout when you were a kid."

"Yeah, that's right—an eagle scout with all the merit badges my little chest could hold. Now just be ready. I'll be there shortly."

As Ben hung up the phone, a smile played about his lips. *Boy scout? That's not exactly true,* he thought. *I just don't like rushing around.* He chuckled a little, thinking of his friend's words. *But if I do run into any little old ladies, I'm their man.*

Ben checked his watch again, then snatched his keys off their hook near the door. "Time to go," he muttered. After checking that the door was properly secured, Ben headed toward the subway platform.

Ivy ran along the sidewalk past the cars of her many wedding guests, her dress bunched in her hands, her beaded pumps slowing her only slightly, her veil trailing behind her. Emotions surged through Ivy; adrenaline fueled her flight from the church. Her vision was partially blurred from tears; why she was crying, she couldn't have said. Relief, guilt, uncertainty, and embarrassment all warred for prominence in Ivy's jumbled thoughts. She only knew as she ran that she needed to get away, far away, before the doors of the church burst open, and people—Keith, mainly—spilled out looking for her.

As she neared the corner, she saw the elevated train platform. She didn't hesitate for an instant— without looking back, she bolted up the stairs to catch the train. She dropped her skirts long enough to slip a couple of the dollars her father had given her into the machine to buy a fare card.

She heard the low rumble of an approaching train. *I've got to get on that,* she thought frantically. *I've got to get away from here.* "Come on, come on," she urged the machine as it processed her money and generated the small card.

After what seemed an eternity, her fare card popped out. She snatched it from the dispenser, gathered her skirts again, and made her way to the platform. Oblivious to the curious stares of her fellow passengers, she struggled to get her billowing wedding confection through the turnstile. As she finally managed to swipe her fare card and ease through, the train she'd heard before was already at the stop, passengers pouring in and out of its doors.

Ivy hurried to the nearest car. As she stepped in, her trailing veil caught on a loose nail in the platform, snatching her head back. She turned to free her veil, and in the rapid motion, got her skirts caught on a handrail inside the train.

As she struggled to free herself, the frustration and emotion of the day churned Ivy's insides, causing fresh tears to spring to her eyes and harsh words to build in her throat.

Well, there's something you don't see every day. Ben looked up from the paper he had been reading when Ivy burst into the train car. Like everyone else who saw her, Ben was struck by the incongruity of the sight of a young woman in full wedding regalia boarding the elevated train. *She must be running late for her wedding,* Ben thought. *But why on earth would she be riding the train . . . don't they usually send limos for the bride?* Questions swirled around in Ben's mind. As he watched, the woman began to struggle with her gown.

Ben's instinct took over, crowding out the questions, propelling him out of his seat to offer assistance.

"Let me help you," he said as he reached out to unsnag to veil. "It's caught outside the doors on the platform. Be still and let me see if I can unhook it without tearing your veil."

Ivy turned from her struggles to face the voice, the sound of ripping fabric accompanying her movements. "I don't care about tearing it," she snapped, panic at the edges of her voice. "I just want to get unstuck before the doors close and crush me to death."

Ben could sense the woman's distress, so he wisely decided that now would not be the time to point out that there was little or no chance of the doors closing on her since a sensor monitored the doors for obstructions. Ben realized that telling her that tidbit of information would most likely annoy her rather than comfort her. So instead, he held his tongue, bent low, and gently released the veil from its tether.

A bing-bong tone filled the air around them, signaling that the train's doors were closing. Ben helped the distressed bride out of the doorway and fully into the train car. Her skirts were still tangled in the handrail. Ben and Ivy bent to unsnare the fabric at the same moment that the train lurched forward. They both stumbled, but Ben was able to regain his footing before he fell down completely. Ivy, however, was not so lucky.

As the train moved forward, Ivy did, too, sprawling completely flat on the floor of the train car. As she fell, her trapped dress stayed put, ripping an enormous jagged tear down the side of the billowing skirts.

Ben quickly knelt to help her up. He carefully lifted her from her prostrate position on the floor. Not surprisingly, tears streamed uncontrollably from her eyes, blending with her makeup to create small rivers of black that coursed down her cheeks and splashed unto the bodice of her dress.

"I'm so sorry," he apologized unnecessarily. "But I'm sure somebody at the church will be able to help you fix your dress before the wedding."

"Not very likely," she muttered as she brushed her cheeks with her sleeves.

Not fully understanding, Ben tried again to comfort her. "Well then I'm sure your groom will be happy to marry you no matter what you're wearing."

Ivy shook her head and chuckled humorlessly. "You have no idea." Slowly gathering the center of her control, Ivy snatched her skirt hard, renting the fabric completely. She bustled past her helper with as much dignity as she could muster, leaving a long strip of white taffeta hanging from the handrail.

Studiously ignoring the open stares from her fellow passengers, Ivy settled on a seat and busied herself with arranging her skirts.

Ben found himself mysteriously intrigued by this disheveled bride. As he watched, she jerked the veil off her head and smoothed her fingers through the myriad twists of black shiny hair that covered her head. Slowly, he approached her and took the seat in front of her.

"Forgive me," he began, "but are you all right?"

Ivy shrugged. "How do I answer that?" She spoke as much to herself as she did to him. "Am I all right? Well, I just made the biggest decision of my life, but I made it in such dramatic fashion that my whole world is going to cave in on me." She looked up at Ben and for the first time noticed his earnest hazel eyes. "So, am I all right? I dunno—the jury's still out on that one."

"Do you think you made the right decision?" Ben asked.

"Yes." Ivy didn't hesitate. "It was absolutely the right decision, but I made it the wrong way."

Ben took in her battered wedding attire with a look and then smiled gently at her. "I can imagine what happened," he said. "I'd guess that when the preacher asked the question, your answer was 'I don't'—right?"

"Close but no cigar," Ivy said. "I never even got that far. I turned and ran out the door instead of walking up the aisle. And I left my poor father to pick up the pieces." Ivy shook her head. "I can't believe I did that."

Ben shrugged. "I'm sure you did what you felt you had to do. If there is anything I can do to help . . ."

Ivy studied him closely. Her gaze raked down from his ball cap-covered head, past his rich honey-colored face, and down his solid torso. She quickly averted her eyes before they could travel any farther south, instead focusing her attention on his face, especially his eyes. In their open, hazel depths, she saw a soul she could trust.

"That's very generous, but I don't even know your name," she replied.

Ben smiled broadly. "Well, that's easy enough to fix." He twisted slightly in his seat and extended his hand. "Benjamin J. Stephens at your service, Miss . . . ?" his voice trailed off in question.

"Pleased to meet you, Benjamin J. Stephens." She shook the extended hand. "I'm Ivy Daniels."

"Hello, Miss Daniels." Ben smiled. "You seem to be having a pretty big day."

Ivy laughed in spite of herself. "That, Benjamin J. Stephens, is an understatement. It's turning out to be a much bigger day than I expected."

The train slowed to a halt, and Ivy checked the station.

"Well, this is where I get off," Ivy sighed.

"Then I guess it's where I get off, too." Ben stood to follow.

"What are you doing?" she asked.

"I'm going to walk you home."

Ivy gave him a shaky smile. "That's really not necessary, Benjamin J. Stephens. I can take it from here."

Ben shook his head. "Now what kind of rescuer would I be if I let you walk home? When Benjamin J. Stephens accepts a job," Ben intoned with mock severity, "he does it all the way."

"Honestly," Ivy protested. "It's really not that far. . . ."

"Then it won't take very long. Now stop arguing with me. I'd never forgive myself if you got caught on a fencepost or something."

Laughing, Ivy shrugged her shoulders. "Come on, then—my place is a couple of blocks away."

Ben took Ivy's elbow and helped her over the train threshold and down the stairs to the street. By tacit agreement, they ignored the curious stares of people they passed, although they were undeniably an unusual pair, she in her tattered wedding finery and he in his baseball cap. As Ivy had promised, her apartment building was near the train station. Her building was one of several similar structures that lined the quiet side street. There were four units housed in the square red brick building. A security door with a buzzer entry panel embedded in the wall next to it stood sentry.

As she was starting up the stoop to approach the door, Ivy suddenly stomped her foot in disgust.

"What's wrong?" Ben asked. Ivy gave him a look. "I mean, besides the obvious," he clarified.

"My keys! I don't have my keys. I was in such a hurry to leave the church, I didn't even grab my purse!" Ivy spat a muffled curse. "Man! This day just keeps getting better and better."

"Calm down," Ben said. "There has to be another way in. Do you have a fire escape or a back porch?"

"Well, yeah, but my apartment is on the second floor," Ivy said.

"Which one?"

Ivy shrugged and pointed to the unit on the upper left-hand side of the building. "There's a fire escape-slash-terrace in the back. But I keep my back door locked, you know."

"No spare keys hidden along the doorjamb or in a potted plant?"

Ivy shook her head, the absurdity of the situation causing her to giggle. "Maybe I should just go back to the church. There's probably somebody still there."

Ben looked at her closely. "If you're serious, I can give you cab fare so you won't have to ride the train."

But Ivy's nervous giggles had consumed her, and she didn't hear his offer. "Oh yeah, that would just be the crowning moment of this whole day," she choked out between breaths. "I could just march back into the church, my dress torn to shreds, and explain that no, I haven't changed my mind . . . I just forgot my keys."

Ben's face grew pensive as his boy scout instincts kicked in. "Or, I could just climb up there and unlock the door so you can go home and collect yourself." He reached for her hand and gave it a reassuring squeeze. "You wait here and I'll be back in a few minutes."

Ivy, taking deep breaths to clear her mind, quickly shook her head. "I'll go around back with you. I feel a little, uh, exposed standing out here on the sidewalk in what's left of my wedding dress."

Ben nodded his understanding, and fell in step behind her as she gathered her skirts and led the way around to the back of the building. She pointed at the fire escape ladder. It was anchored to the building several feet from the ground, placed at that height specifically to discourage people from doing what Ben had planned.

Ben walked up to the ladder and stretched to the fullest extension his five-foot-eleven-inch frame could reach. The ladder was about four inches away from his grasping fingers. He searched through the shrubbery at the base of the building, looking for something he could use to boost himself the necessary distance to reach the ladder.

Ivy watched him quietly, waiting to see if his search would yield anything useful. She felt panic building in her chest, knowing that each passing moment meant angry and disappointed people from the aborted wedding were that much closer to converging on her. Finally, she could take the waiting no longer.

"Come here"—she called out to Ben, who was at the other end of the building—"let me give you a boost." She braced her feet apart, crouched slightly, extended her arms, and locked her fingers together to provide Ben with a step.

He looked at her incredulously. "You must be kidding. I can't . . . you wouldn't be able to hold me." His voice trailed off uncertainly.

"I'm much stronger than I look," Ivy assured him. "Besides, we're running out of time and options here. Just let me give you a quick boost and you can take it the rest of the way."

Ben shook his head in amusement at the sight of Ivy, grim determination etched on her beautiful cocoa features, crouched in a booster stance, yards of billowing white fabric scrunched around her.

"This is crazy," he muttered.

"Then it's perfect for this day," Ivy noted. "Come on, Benjamin J. Stephens. Time's a wastin'."

Ben shrugged and walked over to her. Ivy scooted closer to the building and braced her feet more firmly in the soft grass. "Ready?" he questioned. A quick nod was her response.

Ben took a step back, then sprang toward her waiting hands. He timed his jump so he would use her boost for the briefest possible time, springing from the ground, to her hands, to the ladder against the wall. As he jumped, he reached out for the ladder, grasping the bottom rung. Ivy held her ground, a combination of adrenaline and fitness giving her the strength to boost him up. Ben dangled from the bottom rung for a moment, then began to pull himself up. Ivy stepped back and allowed herself to admire his obvious upper body strength, watching as muscles rippled across his back and down his arms.

Abruptly, she shook her head, angry with herself for her wandering thoughts. *Focus, Ivy!* her mind screamed. *Your life just got complicated enough without adding to it, thank you very much!*

Once Ben got his feet on the ladder rungs, it was a matter of moments before he completed his climb to her second story "fire escape-slash-terrace." He carefully avoided several potted plants that lined the small space. He tried the back door, although she had warned him it would be locked.

"Now what, Spiderman?" Ivy called from the ground.

Ben took stock of his surroundings, his eyes lighting on a slightly opened window to the right of the terrace. He leaned over the railing. "Where's this window go?"

"That's my kitchen, over the sink."

Ben moved closer and studied the window. A screen blocked the opening. He retrieved keys from his pocket and dug around the edges of the screen frame, trying to pry it loose. He managed to lift a corner of the screen away from the window. He pulled at it harder, and the screen frame popped out and clattered to the floor of the terrace.

"Sorry, Ivy," he called. "I think I might have broken your screen."

Ivy waved her hand dismissively. "Can you get in?"

"I think so. You didn't leave any dishes in your sink, did you?"

Ivy grimaced. She hadn't eaten in days; she'd been far too anxious about her impending nuptials. "Um, no," she answered finally, "there shouldn't be any dishes."

Ben grabbed the bottom of the window sash and pushed up. The window slid easily out of his way. The rectangular opening was barely large enough to accommodate him.

Ben shimmied in head first, wriggling slightly to ease his way through the window. After working his upper body in, he grabbed the edge of the counter and pulled himself through completely. A loud crash signaled his entry into the apartment.

"I'm afraid your cookie jar is history." Ben called out the window.

"Just come down and open the door," Ivy yelled in response. "And make it snappy!" She looked around anxiously, expecting a search party from the church any moment. She hurried back around to the front of the building, waiting for Ben to open the door.

She didn't have to wait long; within a few short moments, Ben flung open the security door. With a playfully dramatic flourish, he bent low at the waist as he held the door open for her to enter. Grinning slightly, Ivy lifted her chin and strode regally past him. She started up the stairs, and instead of leaving as she expected, Ben allowed the door to close and began following behind her.

"What are you doing?" Ivy turned on the stairs to face him.

"All a part of the service, ma'am," Ben said easily. "I just want to see you in completely."

Ivy smiled at him and shook her head. "That really isn't necessary—I can take it from here."

Ben hesitated. "Are you sure there isn't something else I can do for you. I hate to leave you like this."

"You are a very kind man," Ivy said sighing, "and you've really done plenty for me today. You've come to my rescue at least twice today, and I really appreciate it."

"But that's enough," Ben tried to read her

thoughts, "and you want me to leave you alone now, right?"

This time Ivy hesitated, staring at a point past Ben at the street in front of her building. Slowly she focused her gaze on the helpful stranger who stood patiently three steps below her. She said nothing for several long moments, trying to take the measure of the man and the situation.

"If you really want to help me," she said finally, "you'll take me away for a while. They'll all be here soon and I'm not ready to face it."

Without a second's hesitation, Ben reached into his wallet and produced the tickets to the ball game. "The Cubs are in town. Wanna go?"

Ivy's face brightened as the first genuine smile she'd felt in hours spread across her face. "That, Benjamin J. Stephens, would be perfect. Just give me a minute to change into something a little more appropriate." Ivy dashed up the stairs to her apartment.

Ben took a seat on the stairs to await her return. *Darryl's gonna kill me about his ticket,* Ben thought briefly. *But this is an emergency—he'll have to understand.*

Why is this an emergency? a contradictory voice inside his head demanded. *You helped her get on the train and into her apartment—why are you involving yourself in this woman's life. Lord knows, girlfriend's got issues.*

Ben imagined the proverbial angel and devil perched on his shoulders as his conscience did battle.

"I helped because it was the right thing to do," Ben muttered. "And I invited her to the game because she seemed like a woman who needed a break."

Sure thing, boy scout, the devilish voice said. *And her needing a break wouldn't have anything to do with the fact that she's probably the most beautiful woman you've ever come in contact with, tears and all—right?*

Ben shook his head defiantly. "Certainly not!" His voice echoed in the stairwell. "I'm just trying to help a sista out."

Yeah, whatever, was the skeptical reply.

Who are you talking to?" Ivy emerged from her apartment dressed in jeans and a T-shirt. "They're not here, are they?"

"Who?" Ben's brow furrowed in puzzlement.

"The search party from the church. They haven't shown up, have they?" Ivy peered worriedly down the stairs toward the street.

"No, no, it's nothing like that," Ben assured her. "I was just talking to myself."

"Oh," Ivy smiled. "Well, you know they say it's OK to talk to yourself as long as you don't answer."

"If that's the case, I'm in deep trouble," Ben grinned in return. "Now, having said that, do you still want to go to the game with me?"

"Benjamin J. Stephens, if you're crazy, then you're the perfect man for this crazy day." After turning to lock her apartment door, Ivy started down the stairs toward him. "Now, take me out to the ball game. Take me out to the crowd."

Chuckling, Ben picked up on the old song she

was quoting. "Buy you some peanuts and Cracker Jacks?"

"I don't care if we never come back!" Ivy dissolved into giggles. She slung her purse over her shoulder and gestured for him to lead the way.

When she raised her arm, Ben caught a glimpse of an adornment on her upper arm. Thinking at first that it was some kind of jewelry, he looked again.

"A tattoo?" He reached for her arm to examine the decoration more closely. Encircling the well-toned bicep on her left arm was an ivy vine tattoo. "This is beautiful," Ben said. "The detail is so intricate." He looked up from the tattoo and regarded Ivy with a new appreciation. "Why didn't I notice this before?"

Ivy pulled her arm gently from his grasp. "Because before I was wearing a wedding gown—a long-sleeved wedding gown." The laughter melted off her face. "Mom insisted on long sleeves—she's never liked the tattoo. Keith never thought much of it either, for that matter, so I agreed to wear long sleeves in June so they wouldn't be embarrassed." Ivy looked away and folded her arms across her body, rubbing absently on the tattoo.

"I'm sorry; I didn't mean to bring you down." Ben gave her a supportive smile. "Try and put all that behind you, at least for a while. Remember," he broke into song, "it's root, root root for the home team, if they don't win it's a shame. . . ."

Ivy joined him and their voices blended to finish

the last line: "Well it's one—two—three strikes you're out at the old ball game!"

Good humor restored, at least for a while, Ivy and Ben left Ivy's apartment and headed to the elevated train station.

Three

The confusion he'd felt when he realized Albert Daniels was standing alone in the doorway of the sanctuary was nothing compared to the white-hot pain that speared Keith Jamison's heart now. Ivy's father had mercifully led Keith out of the sanctuary, away from the questioning stares of the would-be wedding guests. Now the two men were in the pastor's study, the stunned groom sitting with his head in his hands.

"I don't understand," Keith muttered repeatedly. "It doesn't make any sense. . . ." Keith looked up at Albert. "What did she say, Mr. D.? She had to have said something before she ran out on me."

Albert patted the distraught man on the shoulder. "She said she would talk to you herself later, Keith. She'll explain—"

"Explain?" The word burst from Keith's lips as he shot out of his chair. "How can she possibly explain this . . . this . . . humiliation? This betrayal?" Keith's dark-brown eyes shone with unshed tears. "Where did she go?" Keith demanded. "I want to see her now!"

Albert shook his head. "I'm not sure, son. But she promised me she'd talk to you today. Just give her a little time. This wasn't easy for her, either, you know."

Keith's laugh was harsh and humorless. "She wasn't the one left standing at the altar. She's not the one who has to go out there and tell all those people the wedding's off. She's not the one left holding the bag. So forgive me, Mr. D., if I'm having a hard time mustering any sympathy for Ivy."

"Look, Keith, I know you're upset, so I'm going to let it slide," Albert's voice was stern, "but don't you forget that's my daughter we're talking about here. I'm not defending what she did, but I'm not going to let you disrespect her, either."

Keith shook his head slowly. "I'm sorry, Mr. D. You're right, I'm just upset. I love Ivy. I still want to marry her. I just need to talk to her; I need to straighten this out."

A sharp knock on the door interrupted them. "Gentlemen? May I come in?"

Albert opened the door to reveal the pastor. "Please join us, Reverend Timothy." Albert stepped aside to allow the pastor to enter.

"I'm afraid the guests are starting to get a little restless," Rev. Timothy began. "Would you like me to make any announcement? Do you want them to wait, or what?"

A long silence stretched through the room and Albert and Rev. Timothy waited for Keith to respond. Keith crossed to the window and stared out at the packed parking lot. His thoughts were a tangled heap.

What could I possibly say? How can I face those people? I know they're all either laughing at me or feeling sorry for me. Keith frowned. *I couldn't take either of those. I should just run off like Ivy did and let Rev. Timothy handle it.* Keith turned to face the waiting men. He opened his mouth, fully prepared to ask the pastor to make the announcement. Suddenly, he stopped himself. *This is something I have to do,* he decided. *Maybe I can salvage some shred of self-respect if I do.*

"I'll handle it, Reverend Timothy," Keith said finally. "I'll let them all know there's not going to be a wedding here today."

Keith rebuttoned his tuxedo jacket and smoothed the lapels. He took a moment to gather his thoughts, and then after a deep, steadying breath, his jaw set in a hard determined line, he left the pastor's study and reentered the sanctuary.

The low buzz of conversation that permeated the room ended abruptly as the audience realized Keith had returned. He pulled a nearby microphone off its stand and stepped to the center of the front of the church. Clearing his throat, he began.

"Ladies and gentlemen, friends and family, I'm afraid I have some bad news. Unfortunately, it doesn't look like there's going to be a wedding today."

Sharp gasps of surprise and disappointment met his statement.

"Ivy had a little attack of cold feet." Keith's efforts at humor were strained. "But I want you to go on downstairs to the reception. I'll ask the caterers to serve the food and cut the cake. I think we all could use a party right about now." Keith's voice cracked slightly at the end of his words. He turned away quickly and busied himself with putting the microphone back in its stand.

At first, no one in the sanctuary moved. Then the mothers of the bride and groom rushed from their seats toward Keith. The bridesmaids and groomsmen were close behind, until Keith was surrounded by the concerned faces of the wedding party.

"Where's Ivy?" Grace's shrill question rose above the din.

"I don't know, Mrs. D." Keith shrugged. "Apparently she left the church right before she was supposed to walk down the aisle."

"That can't be!" Grace shook her head in disbelief. "We were just talking back in the lounge . . . she was happy, excited."

"I don't know what to say, Mrs. D.," Keith replied over the head of his mother who had him wrapped in a supportive bear hug. "All I know right now is that she is not here—and that she left the church under her own power."

"It's going to be all right, baby," Keith's mother Pat crooned. "Don't worry about a thing. Ivy'll come around . . . she just got scared, that's all."

Pat's sentiments were echoed throughout the tight circle of wedding participants who surrounded Keith. As his groomsmen patted him supportively on the back and shoulders, and Ivy's bridesmaids squeezed his hands and arms sympathetically, Keith could feel himself begin to believe that it was all some kind of misunderstanding, some disconnect he could easily clear up once he had a chance to talk to Ivy.

"I need you guys to lead everyone downstairs to the reception hall." Keith spoke in a low voice, just loud enough to be heard by the wedding party. "Make sure the caterers put out the food, but don't let anybody cut the cake—I'm going to find Ivy and we'll cut our cake together . . . after our wedding!"

"Hey batter, batter, batter—swing!" Ben stood at his seat, his hands cupped around his mouth, taunting the opposing team. The Cubs were winning, and he should have been having a great afternoon. His enjoyment was tempered, however, by the melancholy woman slumped in the seat next to him.

Ben turned from the game to check on Ivy. "The Cubbies are up by two and it's the top of the seventh inning. It's a beautiful, sunny afternoon at the friendliest ballpark in the major league." He ticked off his points with his fingers. "And you look like somebody just ran over your puppy. This trip to the ball game was supposed to cheer you up."

Ivy smiled weakly. "I know. It's not that I don't appreciate the effort—yours and the Cubs'—but I can't stop thinking about . . ." Her voice trailed off. "Well, you know what I'm thinking about."

Ben sat down so he could look her in the eye. "Earlier you said you were sure you had made the right decision. Do you still feel that way?"

"Yes." Ivy didn't hesitate. "It was the right decision. I just made it the wrong way. Keith didn't deserve to be treated that way. I shouldn't have embarrassed him like that just because I changed my mind." Ivy shook her head. "That was just wrong."

Seems to me you did the guy a favor.

"A favor?" Ivy gave him an incredulous look. "How do you figure that?"

"You saved him from being committed to a woman who doesn't truly love him. Everybody deserves to be loved unconditionally. If you weren't going to give him that, then it was right for you to let him go."

Ivy sat quietly for a moment, considering Ben's words. "I didn't think of it like that. . . ."

"Well, you should. Later, that is." Ben signaled a souvenir vendor who was coming toward them. "Now you should put it all out of your mind and concentrate on the game." Ben pointed at the vendor's display and handed the man a bill. This is for you." Ben gave Ivy the souvenir. "If this doesn't help you forget for a while, nothing will."

Ivy smiled broadly as she accepted Ben's offering and turned to focus on the activity down on the field.

The big, blue foam "Number 1" hand Ben bought for her went a long way toward helping Ivy relax and regroup. The Cubs' victorious performance was also a respite for her troubled mind.

But all too soon the game was over, and Ivy and Ben joined the throng that was filing out of the stadium.

"Are you hungry?" Ben asked. There's a great

sandwich shop just a couple of blocks down Clark Street."

Ivy reluctantly shook her head. "Thanks anyway, but it's time for me to face the music."

"It's not time unless you're ready for it to be time," Ben said firmly.

"You're sweet." Ivy gently touched his clean-shaven cheek. "And I have had a very nice time, but I really do have to go."

Ben nodded shortly. "OK, I understand." He gestured in the direction of the El train platform. "Let's go."

Ivy did not even pause at his apparent decision to escort her home. Given what she'd seen of Benjamin J. Stephens in the last few hours, it seemed perfectly natural.

They boarded the train with much less fanfare than earlier in the day. However, Ivy felt herself growing more and more anxious with each passing stop. She was trying to form an explanation, trying to figure out what she would say to Keith to make him understand. The only thing that kept coming to her mind was the truth—that she didn't love Keith. *But should I tell him that?* her mind raced. *Would that just be rubbing salt into the wounds?*

When the train reached her stop, Ben had to nudge her to get her attention.

"This is it," he announced. "Where were you just then? Or do I even have to ask."

"Probably be better if you didn't." Ivy rose to exit the train. "I can take it from here, Ben. I'm sure you have better things to do than walk me home."

"Nope." Ben shook his head. "Not a thing. And don't start. You should know by now that when Benjamin J. Stephens accepts a job—"

"He does it all the way," Ivy finished, laughing. "Yes, I suppose I do know that by now." She lodged no further protest as he followed her off the train.

During the short walk to her apartment building, Ben kept up a steady stream of conversation, covering topics ranging from the Cubs to the weather to the upcoming city council election. Ivy knew what he was doing—and why—and she had yet another reason to be grateful to this kind stranger who had come to her rescue.

No, I suppose I can't still consider him a stranger, she thought. *After all he's done for me today . . . and all he could have done, but didn't.* About a block from her apartment, she stopped in her tracks and studied him carefully. *Even though he broke into my house today, he didn't take advantage of the situation, and he gave me a ticket to the ball game he was obviously holding for someone else. No, he's certainly not still a stranger.*

Ben, oblivious to her sudden stop, continued his running chatter. Seconds later he became aware that he walked alone, then stopped and turned back to her.

"You know what you are, Benjamin J. Stephens?" Ivy pointed the giant blue foam finger at him. "You are a very nice guy." She covered the distance between them in two long strides. "And I am very thankful for your help this afternoon. I don't know what I would have done without you." She leaned up on her toes and brushed his cheek with a soft kiss.

She felt the look of pleased surprise that spread across his face before she saw it. She smiled back at him, and for a moment, the world fell away and there was nothing left but the easy warmth that flowed between them.

Then a car door slammed in the distance, tearing Ivy's attention away from Ben. The smile faded from her face and the foam finger she had been waving at Ben dropped to her side. Ben looked first at her, then at a point farther down the street where her attention was suddenly riveted.

A man wearing a tuxedo and tails stepped away from a fire-engine red BMW and stood in the middle of the sidewalk.

"Keith, I presume?" Ben whispered to Ivy.

She didn't answer or even acknowledge she heard the question. She had resumed walking, but Ben noticed her gait was much slower, bordering on a crawl, and her shoulders slumped. Despite being enveloped by an urge to protect her, Ben held back a few respectful feet.

Here goes nothing, Ivy thought as she approached Keith.

With one long, searing look, Keith took in her jeans, the giant foam finger, and Ben, standing a few feet behind. She stopped a couple of feet away from him. For a few strained moments, no one spoke.

"So, how was the game?"

Ivy hesitated; that was the last thing she had expected Keith to say. "Um, fine," she responded. "The Cubs won seven to five."

"That's nice." He crossed his arms in front of his chest. "And it was certainly worth you running out on our wedding for, right?"

Ivy took a deep breath, stalling to gather her thoughts. "I need to explain—"

"Explain?" The façade of calm Keith projected burned away as his temper flared. "Explain? What possible explanation could you have?" He stepped toward her, his voice rising with every word. "What could possibly justify what you did today, Ivy? What?"

Before Ivy could formulate a response, Ben appeared between them.

"Everything OK, Ivy?" Ben cast a wary eye toward Keith.

"Who the hell is this?" Keith demanded, ignoring Ben to glare at Ivy. "Is this," he gestured disdainfully in Ben's direction, "the explanation you have for me?"

Ben took another step in Keith's direction. Ivy quickly raised her hand, stopping his progress. "This is Ben Stephens, a friend of mine, Keith," Ivy said, "and he has nothing to do with what happened between us."

"A friend?" Keith choked on the words. "How is it that I never met your *friend*? And I suppose he just happened to have tickets for a game today? And you just happened to forget you had a wedding scheduled for the same day as the game. And of course, you had to see the Cubs play—to hell with a wedding! The ball game was much more important. Right?"

"Keith, look, we have a lot to talk about, and sarcasm is not going to help." Ivy stood with her hand still pressed against Ben's chest, silencing him.

"Yes, Ivy," Keith ground out between his teeth, "we do have a lot to talk about. So why don't you tell your *friend* here to get lost so we can talk in private?"

Against her hand, Ivy could feel Ben's heart beating faster and his chest muscles flexing as his breathing grew shallow. She knew, before she even looked, that Keith's words and tone had pushed Ben right to the edge of anger. She turned to Ben, a pleading look on her face.

"It's all right, Ben. I'll be fine . . . you can go now." She hoped her voice sounded stronger than she felt.

"Are you sure?" The question hung in the air.

"She said you can go now, pal." Keith addressed Ben for the first time. "So beat it. This has nothing to do with you."

"Ivy?" Ben studiously ignored Keith, looking instead into Ivy's eyes. "Are you sure you'll be all right?"

"Of course she'll be all right," Keith spat out. "I am her fiancé, not some kind of serial killer. I don't know who the hell you think you are, but you need to back off—now!"

Ivy slowly lowered the hand that had restrained Ben. She returned his steady gaze. "I am fine, Ben.

Thank you for all your help today, but I need to handle this alone."

"*Handle this?*" Keith was outraged. "Is that what I am now, something you have to *handle?*"

Ivy didn't respond to Keith, choosing instead to focus on Ben. "Really, Ben, it's OK." When Ben made no move to leave, Ivy realized she'd have to bring an end to this standoff. She turned her back to Ben and faced Keith. She said firmly, "Let's go upstairs to my apartment so we can talk."

Keith shot one last burning look at Ben, then reached for Ivy's hand. After a brief pause, Ivy slid her hand into his and they started down the sidewalk to her apartment building.

Ben watched them leave, waiting to see if Ivy would look back. When she didn't, he turned and walked toward the train station, his heart much heavier than it had any right to be. "Good luck, Ivy Daniels," Ben muttered. "You're going to need it."

Four

"How could you do this to me, Ivy?" Keith's agitated pacing made her small living room seem even smaller. "Do you have any idea how humiliating that was?"

Ivy sat on her couch, watching Keith's aimless trek back and forth across the room. "All I can say is I'm sorry. It was not my intention to humiliate you."

"Sorry? All you can say is sorry?" Keith stopped in front of the couch, towering over her with six feet of simmering anger. "No, I think you can say a little more than sorry."

"What, Keith? What can I say that will make this all right for you?" Ivy looked up at him, a swirl of mixed emotions surging through her. Despite his obvious anger and frustration, she felt no fear. She was confident that Keith was no threat to her, even under these circumstances. A tinge of remorse colored the stronger feelings of pity that filled her soul. She was truly sorry, if not for her decision, then for the way she made it. She pitied Keith, and in a bigger sense her parents, who were surely embarrassed by the day's events. And she felt confused. Because in this moment, when her focus should be on Keith and her aborted wedding, thoughts of the kind and sensitive Ben kept invading her mind.

"Are you even listening to me, Ivy?" Keith demanded. "Tell me why. You owe me at least that much. Tell me why you did this."

This is it, she thought. *The truth, or a gentle lie?* "It was me, Keith." She decided to split the difference. "I just wasn't ready. I suddenly realized the commitment I was making before God and our families, and I just couldn't do it. I wasn't ready."

"Not ready? Ivy, I don't understand. We have been dating for over two years. How could you not be ready?" The anger slowly drained from Keith. His voice was plaintive, his eyes pleading. "Come back to the church with me. They're all still there, waiting for us. Please Ivy, won't you marry me?"

Ivy was stunned into silence. Thoughts formed in her head faster than she could give voice to them. Finally after a few dazed moments, she stammered, "What do you mean they're still at the church?"

"I told them all to wait. I told them we'd be back once this misunderstanding was cleared up." Keith dropped to one knee before her. "Don't humiliate me twice in one day, Ivy. You have to come back with me."

"But they can't still be at the church . . . I left hours ago," Ivy managed. "Keith, you shouldn't have done that. . . ." Her voice trailed off.

"Why not? I knew you'd come to your senses soon enough. You just got cold feet, Ivy. That's all. It happens to every bride. Don't make a big deal out of it." Keith's tone grew impatient as he stood from his kneeling position. "Come on, now. We need to get back. They won't wait all day, you know."

Ivy looked at him as if he had suddenly taken leave of his senses. "I am not going back to the church with you. And you shouldn't have had them wait at all. It's not going to happen, Keith. Not today." *Maybe not ever. . . .*

"What do you expect me to say to them?" Keith demanded. "You expect me to go back to that church and tell them—again—that there is not going to be a wedding? How can you do that to me again?"

"I'm not going to let you pressure me, or shame me, or guilt me into marrying you. You deserve better than that; and if you don't, I certainly do." Ivy spoke with a conviction that surprised her. "Now I can call the church and explain what's going on to the pastor. He'll tell them if you'd prefer."

"Yeah . . . you do that. 'Cause I'm not cleaning up any more of your messes today." Keith stalked to the door. "And understand, Ivy, that this is not over . . . not by a long shot. You mean too much to me for me to let it end this way."

With that, Keith slammed out of her apartment. Ivy heaved a sigh and climbed off the couch to lock the door behind him. *That went well,* she thought, leaning her forehead against the door. "I guess I need to call the church." Her voice filled the silence. She was crossing the room to get the phone book when a knock sounded at her door.

What now, Keith, she thought blackly. *What else is there to say?* She slowly pulled open the door, bracing herself for another argument.

"Ivy honey, what have you done?"

Ivy's eyes widened in surprise as her mother swept into the room, her father close behind.

"How did you get in?" In Ivy's security-conscious building, visitors had to call on the intercom and wait to be admitted through the locked entry door.

"We passed Keith on his way out. He let us into the building." Grace shook her head disapprovingly at her daughter. "He was very upset, Ivy. How could you?"

"I'm fine, Mommy. Thanks for asking." Ivy closed the door and leaned back against it.

Albert extended his arms toward her. Ivy gratefully walked into the hug her father offered. "It's going to be all right, Ivy," he soothed.

Grace crossed her arms in front of her chest. "Well, you're obviously all right," she huffed. "But where have you been? And how are you going to fix this situation?"

Ivy released her father and turned to face her mother. "Mom, why don't you have a seat, and we'll talk." Ivy moved to the couch and patted a place next to her for Grace to sit.

Grace settled on the couch and reached for her daughter's hands. Holding Ivy's hands tightly between her own, Grace looked earnestly into Ivy's eyes.

"I don't understand, honey. Keith was such a great catch. How could you let him go?"

Ivy took a deep, steadying breath before attempting to answer. "Mom, it's a little more complicated than that."

"More complicated? What is it, Ivy? Tell me," Grace urged.

"Mom, I realized I just don't love Keith—not the way a wife should love her husband." Ivy looked deeply into her mother's eyes, praying she'd find some understanding there.

"But you were together for two years," Grace said. "Did you just realize now you didn't love him?"

"I thought I loved him, Mom. I really did. I tried to love him. But what I feel for Keith is not enough to sustain me for the rest of my life." Ivy's voice took on a pleading tone. "Once I understood that, then I really had no choice."

Grace shook her head. "There is always a choice, Ivy. You chose to embarrass yourself, your family, Keith, and his family."

"Grace!" Albert was shocked by his wife's words. "You're being too hard on her. If she didn't love him, then she did the right thing."

Grace's eyes narrowed as she turned her wrath on her husband. "She did not do the right thing! She should have married Keith. He is a wonderful young man, and he loves her completely." Grace turned back to her daughter. "You're looking for a fairy tale, Ivy, and it doesn't exist. The best anybody can hope for is a good, honest, stable man who loves you and is willing to provide for you. Love comes and goes. It's an illusion."

Albert's jaw dropped in astonishment. "Grace?

Do you hear what you're saying? Love is an illusion?"

Grace waved her hand dismissively in his direction, ignoring the crestfallen look on his face. "What I'm saying is stability, honesty, fidelity are the things that really count. That's what makes a good life and a good marriage. And Ivy, you foolishly threw all that away today."

Albert said nothing further, apparently conceding the point to his wife.

Watching her parents' interaction, Ivy shook her head sadly, feeling tears well up in her eyes.

"Mom, I had hoped you would be more understanding. I don't believe love is an illusion. I believe love is a real power in the universe that fills up a person until there is no space for doubts or insecurities. And Mom, unless and until I feel that kind of love, I'm not going to marry anybody."

"Then I guess you've decided to live a solitary life," Grace snapped. "Because Prince Charming exists only in the movies."

When he returned to the El train platform, Ben knew he had a stop to make before heading home. "I've got some 'splainin' to do."

"Ben! You're alive!" Darryl Moore flung open the door of his apartment and rushed out into the hall. He grabbed Ben's hand and pumped it enthusiastically.

Ben, bemused by Darryl's greeting, regarded his friend curiously. "Of course I'm alive. What are you talking about?"

"I figured you had to be dead." Darryl dropped Ben's hand. "That would be the only possible explanation for why you didn't show up here with my Cubs ticket." Darryl's tone was accusing.

"I know, man. That was messed up," Ben apologized. "But I can explain, if you let me in."

Darryl shrugged. "I doubt you can explain, but I'm curious, so come on in." He held the door open. "How was the game, by the way?"

Ben entered the apartment and turned to face his friend. "What makes you think I went?"

"Call it a hunch," Darryl muttered. "So, how was it?"

"The Cubs won."

Darryl made a knowing sound.

"But that's not the most important part," Ben said hurriedly. "This has been a very interesting afternoon."

"Oh, has it? I wouldn't know; I've been here all day, waiting for my boy to show up with my ticket."

"Hold up a second, man. Let me explain." Ben launched into a detailed telling of his encounter with the runaway bride, and the series of events that unfolded after that.

"So you see, Darryl, I really had no choice. The lady was in trouble and needed my help."

"Your help maybe, but did she need my ticket, too?" Darryl's anger was cooling, but he still wasn't quite ready to let Ben off the hook.

Ben shrugged. "It was the only thing I could think of at the time. She asked me to get her out of there, and the ball game seemed the most logical escape." Ben gave Darryl an apologetic look.

"I'm really sorry, man. I promise I'll make it up to you. Next game's on me."

"Man, I can't believe you gave my ticket away."

"You didn't see her, Darryl. She was distraught and crying and panicked and trapped." Ben's voice softened. "You would have done the same thing."

Darryl snorted at that.

"I'm serious, man," Ben insisted. "You would have had to help her, too."

"Maybe . . . ," Darryl allowed. "What'd she look like?"

"What?"

"You heard me, hommie. What'd she look like?" Darryl studied Ben closely.

"She, uh, she looked . . . sad," Ben answered finally. "And by the time we got the dress out of the door, she looked a little raggedy."

"No way . . . that's not a description." Darryl shook his head. "Now I'll try again—what'd she look like?"

Ben sighed in exasperation. "Come on, Darryl. What do you want me to say? She is short—five-foot three or four, I'd guess. She has the prettiest cocoa-colored skin I've ever seen. Her hair is jet black and she wears it in—not locks, really—but some kind of twisty style. From the looks of her arms, she works out. Oh, and she has the most amazing tattoo—"

"A tattoo?"

"Yeah, but it's not manly or anything like that. She's got a vine of ivy going around her upper arm." Ben paused, remembering. "It's really kinda sexy."

"Oh, I'm starting to get the picture now," Darryl smirked. "Your damsel in distress was a hottie, so you blew me off for her—right?"

Ben was quick to protest. "It was nothing like that," he retorted. "Her looks had nothing to do with it."

"Right—and I'm Michael Jordan," Darryl laughed. "Try that line on somebody else, hommie. I know you too well, and you can't tell me that if you'd run into the same situation but the girl was a dog, you would have still given her my ticket."

"Unlike you, I don't make my decisions based on how somebody looks," Ben snapped. "There is so much more that matters."

"Uh-huh." Darryl sounded skeptical. "Like what? What led you to make the decision to give away my ticket?"

"Man, I have already said I'm sorry. How long you gonna keep beating that horse?"

"Oh, I'm over it—you're right, next game's on you." Darryl shook his head. "No, this is about something else. I want to hear about the *much more* you're talking about."

Instead of answering, Ben crossed the apartment to the kitchen. He opened the refrigerator and pulled out a pair of beer bottles. He twisted off the caps and handed one of the bottles to Darryl. Then, Ben grabbed one of the dinette chairs and spun it around. He threw one leg over the chair, straddling it as he settled down. After a long drag of beer, Ben was ready to answer Darryl's query.

"I can't really explain it, Darryl. She was certainly beautiful, but it wasn't that. She seemed to be in so much trouble . . . it was like she had been trapped, but she was finally breaking free. She was vulnerable and proud and determined and frightened all at the same time." Ben shook his head slowly. "I was . . ." He paused, searching for the right word. "Captivated. Within five minutes of meeting her, I would have done anything for her."

"To help her, you mean," Darryl interjected. "You would have done anything to help her, right?"

Ben focused on his friend as if suddenly realizing he was still sitting there. "Yeah, of course. Help her—that's what I meant."

Darryl sipped his beer. " 'Cause if you mean anything else, my brother, you are heading for trouble."

"Anything else like what?" Ben feigned ignorance.

"Don't fall for this girl, Ben. She's got issues."

Ben laughed humorlessly. "Funny, I was thinking exactly the same thing earlier this afternoon."

"Then you know I'm telling the truth. Forget about this Ivy," Darryl warned. "Believe me, you'll be a fool if you don't."

"Aw, man. You don't have to worry about me." Ben lifted his bottle in mock salute. "Benjamin J. Stephens is nobody's fool."

"Yeah," Darryl said skeptically. "I hear ya talkin'."

Keith eased the red BMW into its reserved parking space behind his apartment building and turned off the engine. He folded his arms along the top of the steering wheel and rested his head against his arms. *What now?* he thought. *This can't be happening to me. Not to me! How will I ever be able to show my face again?* A great sigh tore through him as he struggled to control the bubble of despair building in his throat. *We were so good together, and now this? I don't understand. . . .*

A sharp rapping on the passenger side window roused him from his thoughts. He lifted his head to see who it was. He turned the key one notch so he could lower the power window.

"What are you doing here?" he asked. "I thought you'd all still be at the church."

"Ivy's dad sent everyone home. He said he was sure there would be no wedding today."

Keith snorted and shook his head. "Guess he had more information than I did. Typical." He turned his attention back to the window. "But what are you doing *here*? Why didn't you just go home? You must be ready to get out of that bridesmaid's dress by now."

"I thought you could use a friend right about now. Can I get in there with you, or do I have to keep talking to you through the window?"

Keith shrugged and hit the power lock button. "Suit yourself. But as you might imagine, I'm pretty lousy company at this moment."

"I'll take my chances." The car door opened and there was a moment of rustling as Keith's guest maneuvered her gown into the car. "I can only imagine what you must be feeling," she offered.

"Mainly, I'm confused. I don't know why she did it." He shot a pointed look at the woman in the passenger seat. "You didn't have anything to do with this, did you?"

"Keith! How could you think I'd do something like that?" she pouted. "I would never betray your confidence. You know me better than that."

"I know," he backed down. "I'm sorry. I'm just trying to make sense of it all. You know when I finally found her, she had been to a baseball game with some guy I've never seen before."

"Really?" Shock, disbelief, and something slightly mercenary tinged the word. "How did that happen?"

"I don't know. It's another of the day's unsolved mysteries." Keith leaned back against the padded headrest and closed his eyes. Almost immediately, he felt soft hands gently massaging his temples.

"It's going to be all right," she crooned. "All things happen for a reason."

Keith reveled in the soothing sensations created by her fingertips. He felt some of the day's tension start to flow from his body.

"What are you going to do now?" she asked.

"Ummmm?"

"What's your plan?" she repeated.

Keith sat up, ending the massage. "I don't really know. I'm supposed to be on my way to Maui in the morning for my honeymoon. I've taken the next week off work and everything."

"I think you should go," she said.

"What?"

"Why not? It's already paid for, and I remember you telling me it's nonrefundable. You have already taken off work, packed, got your traveler's checks. . . ." She ticked off the points on her fingers. "I say go. You deserve a vacation, don't you?"

Keith was quiet, considering her suggestion.

"And if you'd like, I could go with you."

The words hung in the air between them for several long moments. Finally, Keith cleared his throat uneasily. "That would be a little difficult, don't you think?"

"No," she insisted. "I've got some time coming to me at work. And Lord knows I could use a little vacation, too."

"I didn't mean difficult because of your job," Keith clarified. "I mean because of . . . well, you know . . . what will people say? What will Ivy say?"

"What do you care what Ivy says? She left you at the altar. I thought the relationship was over."

"Well it's not," Keith said tersely. "It's not over by a long shot." Anger seethed through Keith again. After a moment, he took a deep breath and regained his control. "You know, Maui is a good idea. . . . Yes, I'll go—alone," he looked pointedly at her, "and take the time to regroup. When I get back, Little Miss Ivy will have had a chance to miss me, and she'll be ready to see the light."

The woman next to him shook her head sadly. "Why don't you let it go, Keith. Didn't you say she was with someone else when you found her? What are you holding on to? There are so many other opportunities—right under your nose—that you're missing because of Ivy."

"I don't want any other *opportunities*. I want Ivy. And I will have her—just wait and see."

Five

When the buzz of her intercom sounded throughout her apartment, Ivy's first instinct was to ignore the call. *It's Keith, or Mom, or one of my girls . . . none of whom I want to talk to this morning,* she thought. She had had a long, sleepless night, and she was not ready to face the fallout just yet. She sat at the counter in her kitchen, dressed in cotton pj's, nursing a cup of hot tea. Her stomach had not been feeling quite normal since the drama of the day before, and she was afraid to try to keep down anything more substantial than the tea.

The buzzer sounded again, more insistently this time. *If I don't answer,* she inwardly sighed, *they'll never go away.*

She pushed away from the counter and padded over to the intercom. "Go away," she barked into the speaker. "I'm not feeling up to company this morning."

"Ivy? It's Ben. I just wanted to check on you, make sure you were OK."

Ivy released the talk button on the intercom and stepped back in surprise. *Ben?* The name exploded in her mind. *What on earth is he doing here?*

The buzzer sounded again, startling Ivy out of

her contemplation. She took a deep breath and pushed the talk button.

"I'm sorry, Ben," she managed. "It's just that you were the last person I expected to find at my door today."

"I know," the disembodied voice floated through the intercom. "But I was worried about you. You had quite a day yesterday."

Ivy laughed in spite of herself. "There's an understatement if ever I heard one."

The intercom was silent for a moment. Then the sound of Ben clearing his throat was broadcast into her apartment.

"Um, Ivy? Can I come up, or are we going to have this conversation through the speaker?"

"Oh—of course. Where is my head?" Ivy pressed the button to unlock the security door. As soon as she judged he would have had enough time to enter the building, Ivy released the button, spun, and ran into her bathroom to make herself presentable. She grabbed a thick, colorful chenille robe off a hook on the door and quickly shrugged into it. As she tied the belt tightly around her waist, Ivy checked the mirror above the sink. She ran her fingers through the shiny black twists on her head, accepting that there wasn't much she could do about their disarray. She snatched her toothbrush out of its cup, and quickly brushed her teeth. As she turned off the faucet, she heard Ben's knock at the door. After one last check in the mirror, Ivy left the bathroom and crossed the apartment to the door. She opened the door just as Ben was raising his knuckles for another knock.

"Oh, hi," he said, lowering his hand. "I thought you had changed your mind."

"I was in the back," she said by way of explanation, "trying to make myself suitable to be around decent people. As you said, yesterday was quite a day, and last night was quite a night."

"I'm really sorry to hear that," Ben said. "Did that guy Keith give you a hard time?"

Ivy shrugged and held the door open for Ben to enter. "No harder than I expected or deserved. But it wasn't just Keith. My parents stopped by, too."

"That couldn't have been pleasant, either." Ben walked in, taking great care to keep his back turned away from her.

Ivy watched his movements curiously. "No," she answered slowly, "no, it wasn't." She closed the door and tried to peek around Ben's back. When he turned away from her again, she put her hands on her hips and gave him a look.

"What ya got, Ben?"

Ben smiled sheepishly. "I bought you a little something." He presented her with a medium-sized box. "I happen to know you need one of these."

Ivy accepted the package slowly. "You didn't need to do this. You've done enough for me already. . . ."

"Just open it," he insisted.

She lifted the lid, and inside the box, wrapped in pink tissue paper, was a teddy bear-shaped ceramic cookie jar. She lifted the cookie jar from the box, a smile brightening her face. "But why—"

"It's to replace the one I broke yesterday," he

said. "A kitchen's not complete without a cookie jar."

"I don't know what to say," she mumbled. "This is so sweet . . . you seem to be the only person I know who isn't coming down on me for what happened yesterday."

"Maybe because I'm the only person you know who saw how upset you were yesterday," Ben offered. "Your parents didn't understand?"

Ivy placed the cookie jar on the coffee table and gestured for Ben to sit down. He sat on the sofa, while Ivy settled in a matching chair on the opposite side of the coffee table. "My dad understood—but then again, he has always supported me unconditionally. My mom was another story. She was almost as pissed off as Keith was."

"Why?"

Ivy paused, considering the question. "I don't really know why—" Abruptly, she stopped speaking and looked at Ben. "You don't want to hear all this. You've had enough of my little dramas to last you a lifetime."

Ben smiled gently at her. "Ivy, I would not have come here if I felt that way. I want to help you however I can."

"But why?" Ivy asked. "Why do you care? You don't even know me."

"Yes, I do." Ben nodded. "I know you are courageous and decisive, and I know you could use a friend. Somebody who's in your corner; somebody who won't judge or condemn, somebody who will just listen and understand."

Ivy stared at him, confusing emotions swirling inside her. *He's so sweet! It would be so easy to fall for him,* she thought. She shook her head, scattering the dangerous thoughts. *Oh, how can I even be thinking like that? As if I don't already have enough going on!*

"Ben," she said finally, "you're a really nice guy, but I feel like I have to be clear with you. I couldn't possibly get involved with anyone right now. My life is just too complicated."

Ben shook his head. "You misunderstood. I just want to be your friend, Ivy Daniels. That's all."

Ivy studied him carefully, trying to gauge his sincerity. After a moment, she made a decision. "Benjamin J. Stephens, you just made a new friend."

"Excellent!" Ben's smile seemed to light his whole body. "So what would my new friend like to do today?"

Ivy hesitated. "Actually, I'm supposed to be on my way to Maui today for my honeymoon, but that's not going to happen, huh?" She chuckled humorlessly. "I don't know . . . I guess I sort of figured I'd stay home and keep my head down for a while."

"Nonsense! You have nothing to keep your head down about," Ben declared. "Ivy, don't forget, you did that guy a favor. Sure, maybe you messed up everyone's plan for a party, but people wanting you to have a wedding has nothing to do with you wanting to have a *marriage*." He looked straight into her eyes. "Because when the party is over, the cake has been cut, and the bouquet has been tossed, you are the only one who has to deal with the life that goes on afterwards. And if you weren't ready to be a wife, in addition to being a bride, then walking out was the bravest thing you could have done."

Ivy shifted uncomfortably in her chair. She tore her eyes away from Ben's earnest penetrating stare. "You keep making me out to be this courageous heroine when nothing could be further from the truth. I was not brave . . . not at all." She pushed out of the chair and crossed the room to stare out the window. She hugged herself as if to ward off a chill. "It was fear and panic, plain and simple, that drove me from that church. I bolted because I was afraid of giving my life to a man I didn't love." Turning from the window, she glared defiantly at Ben. "If I was all that brave, I would have figured my feelings out long ago and stopped the wedding before it even began. Could've saved a lot of people a lot of trouble."

Ben leaned forward, resting his elbows on his knees. "You need to stop beating up on my new friend like that, because I'm not going to stand for it much longer. You saved a couple of lives yesterday, Ivy—yours and his. Now, suppose you go get dressed and we get out of here for a while?"

Ivy shook her head slowly. "I really don't think I'm ready to face the world yet."

Ben stood and walked over to her. "Ivy, you really need to get out of here. Look around you—a whole corner of your apartment is filled with wedding presents you are probably going to send back; your suitcases are sitting by the door, reminding you of the honeymoon you aren't going to take; and unless I miss my guess, shortly your phone will be ringing off the hook with your friends calling to check on you, which means you are going to have to talk about yesterday over and over again." He held out his hand to her. "C'mon, let's go outside and play."

"Where would we go?"

"The Taste of Chicago is going on this weekend down at Grant Park. Sundays are always great days at the Taste. Lots of music and other entertainment going on."

Ivy shook her head. "I don't know about that. I'm not sure I'm ready to face anybody."

"Then the Taste is the perfect place to be. There'll be a million people in the park, most of them tourists. The chances of you seeing somebody you know are slim to none." Ben shrugged. "On the other hand, if you stay here . . ."

As if on cue, Ivy's phone rang. Ben cocked an "I told you so" eyebrow at her. Ivy laughed in spite of herself.

"Yeah, I see your point. Give me fifteen minutes." Ignoring the phone, she hurried to her bedroom to dress.

"Where are you going?" The voice was still groggy from sleep, or lack of it.

"I'm going to Hawaii, remember?" Keith sat in a chair across the room from the bed, tying his shoelaces.

"Were you even going to wake me before you left?" The woman sat up in bed, making no move to cover her nakedness.

"Of course," Keith said smoothly. "I just didn't want to disturb you yet, that's all."

"Tell me again why you won't take me to Hawaii with you."

Keith sighed. "It would be too controversial. Ivy would never take me back if I did that."

"Ivy is never going to take you back period, Keith."

"You know I don't believe that. Ivy just needs a little time, then she'll see the light." Keith stood and pulled on his tuxedo jacket.

"And what would Miss Ivy say if she knew where you spent last night? Where you've spent many nights over the last year or so? Would she see the light then?"

Keith's eyes narrowed. "Ivy won't ever know that, will she? I mean, forget what she'll think of me— what is she going to think of you?" He crossed the room and bent to retrieve the crumpled rose-colored chiffon bridesmaid gown from the floor. "After all, you're one of her best friends, right?" He tossed the dress at her. "I don't understand your attitude. I thought we agreed that our, um, association would end after the wedding."

"After the wedding being the operative phrase. At the risk of stating the obvious, you didn't get married."

"Yet. I didn't get married yet."

"Keith"—her tone had a pleading edge to it— "when I realized there wasn't going to be a wedding, I thought—I hoped—that meant it would be our time. I know we agreed to end it after the marriage—I don't want to hurt Ivy any more than you do, but she gave you up. Why can't we . . . ?"

Keith reached out and placed his fingers against her lips. "You have been a wonderful friend to me. But last night shouldn't have happened. I think it's best if we don't see each other, you know, like this again. I need to focus my attention on winning Ivy back."

The woman sprang from the bed and flung the bridesmaid dress onto the floor. "Ivy, Ivy, Ivy! I am sick of hearing that name! Let's see you win her back after she finds out about us!" She stalked across the room and snatched a robe from her closet. "What have I been to you all this time, Keith? Some sort of plaything? Some sort of booty call you can make whenever you feel like it?"

"That's not fair. I have always been very clear about my feelings. I love Ivy. I want to marry Ivy."

"I very much doubt that," she sneered. "You have certainly not been acting like a man in love."

"You are very special to me, too." Keith crossed the room and gathered her in his arms. She stood stiff and unyielding. "I have to fix things with . . . her. There has to be a wedding, or I'll never be able to show my face in this town again. Please try to understand. She humiliated me. I won't be treated that way." He stroked her hair as he spoke, trying to ease the anger from her. "And you should forget about telling Ivy anything about us." The woman stiffened in his arms again, but Keith pulled her closer until she was pressed full against him. "Because not only will Ivy and all your other girlfriends turn against you; I would never be able to forgive such a betrayal. I would never be able to look at you or touch you again. I would hate you until the end of time."

He pulled back and cupped her face in his hands. Then he began to kiss her. She resisted at first, trying to turn her head away from his seeking lips. But he persisted, and slowly the kiss changed from "seek and destroy" to a consensual, all-consuming inferno that scorched the hurt and anger out of her.

Having made his point, Keith pulled away, ending the kiss. "Everything works out the way it's meant to. You must be patient, and let whatever will be, be."

She could only nod weakly, her voice not yet returned.

"I have to go now; I have a plane to catch." Keith stroked his palm against her cheek. "I'll talk to you when I get back. Make sure you stay out of trouble."

She chose not to answer, nuzzling against his hand instead. Then he was gone, closing the bedroom door soundlessly behind him.

She stood stone-still in the center of the room, her lips still tingling from the kiss. *He's right . . . I can't risk losing everything—including Keith—by telling Ivy the truth.* She squared her shoulders. *OK, Keith,* she thought. *We'll play it your way for now. And even if you're still in denial, I know Ivy will never take you back . . . then you'll be mine.*

Six

It was a picture perfect Sunday, and as Ben had predicted, Grant Park was teeming with people attending the Taste of Chicago. Tents erected for the event covered the park, housing countless restaurants that sold samples of their menu offerings. Four stages were stationed at the four corners of the park, each hosted by a different radio station, each offering a different type of music. Scattered throughout the park, street musicians played for pockets of appreciative listeners who tossed money into buckets, hats, or open guitar cases.

Ben led a slightly hesitant Ivy into the park after stopping to purchase a stack of food tickets.

"Whoa, buddy," Ivy protested, "who's gonna eat that much food? You've got enough tickets to feed a small army."

Ben laughed. "Bet you a dollar they're all gone before we leave. I don't know about you, but I'm hungry. And the places I like to eat usually take several tickets. Now, how about some cheesecake?"

"Dessert first?" Ivy wagged her finger at him. "Benjamin J. Stephens, I'm surprised at you."

"Dessert is the best part of the meal. Why not start with the good stuff and work your way back?"

Ben grinned mischievously. "How often have you finished eating and then not had room for dessert? This way, there's always room, and if sometimes that means you don't have room for your veggies, well then that's life."

"Dessert is the reward you get for eating all your veggies," Ivy declared. "You have to earn that cheesecake; you can't just skip to it."

Ben cocked his head at her. "Do you always play it by the book, Ivy Daniels? Do you always do what you're told?" He reached for her hand and placed several meal tickets in her palm. "Come on, live on the edge, break the rules. Have some cheesecake with me."

"But it's eleven o'clock in the morning." She tried a different tack. "We should be looking for pancakes and eggs, not cheesecake."

Ben shook his head and shrugged. "Look, if you don't want any cheesecake, don't get any cheesecake. But make sure you're not getting it because you don't want it, not because of some arbitrary rule you think you have to obey." He released her hand. "I, on the other hand, hear that chocolate chip cheesecake calling my name." He pointed at a bakery booth and then headed in its direction.

Ivy watched him meld into the crowd. *What the hell,* she decided finally. *I've been breaking all kinds of rules this weekend . . . what's one more?* She set off to join him at the bakery booth.

"That's just wrong," she said sternly, pointing at the chocolate chip cheesecake heaped on his plate.

Ben looked from his plate to her, mild dismay

etched on his honey-colored face. "Sorry you feel that way. . . ."

"The caramel apple is much better," she smiled. She stepped past him to the bakery counter and placed her order. Once she received her dessert, she rejoined him. "Let's hear it for the power of cheesecake." She lifted her plate as if making a toast.

Ben shook his head. "Let's hear it for the power of independent thought." He returned her plate toast.

"Hear, hear." Ivy nodded and tapped her plate against his. "And since we're thinking independently this morning, do you suppose there's a booth around here someplace where I can get a big, greasy Italian sausage sandwich? I mean, if I'm going to break the rules, let's break them completely. Who cares about cholesterol and calories?"

"Absolutely." Ben quickly consulted the park map he'd been given when he bought the food tickets. "Looks like there's Italian sausage straight ahead on the left."

Nibbling on their cheesecake, the pair set off in search of the second course of this unorthodox meal.

"Have you talked to her?"

"The last time I saw Ivy, she was in a wedding gown waiting for her father to escort her down the aisle. I haven't talked to her since."

The phone line hummed as the two women considered their next move. "Kim, we have to find her. Don't you think she probably needs to talk about yesterday?"

Kim shook her head. "I don't know, Cherise. If she wanted to talk, she would have called one of us. She has to know we are worried about her. And yet none of her best friends—her bridesmaids, for God's sake—have heard from her. I say we don't crowd her."

"I disagree." Cherise heaved an exasperated sigh. "Kim, we need to round up all the girls and go over to her place. Maybe the reason none of us has heard from her is because she's embarrassed. If that's the case, she needs to know we're in her corner."

"And you think the best way to accomplish that is to round up the posse and swoop in on her?" Kim paused, considering. "I don't know, Cherise. Sounds risky to me."

"But it's not," Cherise insisted. "She's probably alone in that apartment, nursing her wounds, needing to be surrounded by friends. Look, I'm going to call Danielle on my threeway, and you call Trina on yours. Let's have a conference call and get everybody's opinion."

"OK," Kim said, a hesitant note tingeing the word. A few moments and a few click-dial-clicks later, the phone lines buzzed with the conversation between Kim and the would-be bridesmaids.

"OK, what's up?" The voice belonged to Danielle. "I was on my way to church."

"You late, ain't you?" Kim teased. "It's almost noon."

"Better to go late than not to go at all, *Kim,*" Danielle shot back.

"Sorry Danielle, but I thought this was important," Cherise said. "I'm worried about Ivy."

"Well, who isn't?" Trina asked. "Sista, girl's got a lot to be worried about."

Kim chuckled. "Say that, girlfriend! But Cherise is concerned because none of us has heard from Ivy since she left the church."

"What is there for her to say?" Danielle asked. "She ran out on the wedding—I'm sure she believed she was doing what she had to do."

"I think so, too," Kim agreed.

"But don't you all think she's probably upset? I just feel like as her friends and bridesmaids we need to go and be with her," Cherise declared. "We didn't hesitate to converge on her before the wedding when we were having showers and luncheons and bachelorette parties. I think she needs us even more now, and we need to be there for her."

"She's got a point," Trina chimed in. "Maybe we should go by her place and check on her."

"I can't go right now," Danielle said. "I was on my way out the door for church."

"God'll forgive you if you miss a Sunday to help a friend," Kim assured her. "I agree with Cherise—we need to go be with Ivy, let her know she's not alone."

"Yeah, OK, I'll go," Danielle conceded. "But shouldn't we call first? I would hate to miss church and she not even be there."

"Where's she gonna go?" Trina asked.

"Besides," Cherise added, "I've been calling her all morning and she doesn't answer her phone."

"Doesn't that prove she doesn't want to be bothered?" Danielle demanded. "I'm sure she's got some things to sort out, like why she ran out on one of the finest brothers in Chicago."

"That's not very supportive, Dani," Kim chided. "Where's your Christian spirit?"

"Look, we can argue about this later," Cherise interrupted. "Right now we need to decide what time we're going to meet at Ivy's."

"So we decided to go, I take it?" Kim asked.

"Yes," Cherise was firm. "We owe it to Ivy to check up on her. Now can everybody meet in front of Ivy's building in an hour?"

A general chorus of agreement met that request. The bridesmaids said their good-byes and hung up, each going off to attend to whatever details had to be handled before she could go to Ivy's apartment.

A reggae band played on one of the stages positioned in the park. Ben and Ivy stood in front of the stage, bouncing to the beat along with the rest of the audience. Ben found his attention focused not on the band, but instead on the woman standing next to him. He stole surreptitious glances at her, appreciating the way the black twists of hair atop her head shone in the sun, admiring her petite, well-honed figure, and marveling yet again at the bold tattoo encircling her upper arm.

What's your story, Ivy Daniels? he wondered. *A*

woman who gets a tattoo, runs out on her wedding, and yet hesitates to defy the simplest of rules—like eating dessert first. He shook his head slightly. *You seem to be a real contradiction . . . which Ivy is the real Ivy?*

"What?" Her question rose above the music, breaking into his thoughts.

"What what?" Ben repeated, a little confused.

"You're staring at me . . . why?" Ivy drew back unconsciously.

"I didn't mean to stare," Ben began. "It's just that you are such a mystery to me. I was just trying to figure out the enigmatic Ivy Daniels."

"I'm not such a mystery. In fact, you know more of my secrets than anyone . . . especially about yesterday." A faraway look appeared in her eyes. "Except for Keith and my parents, I haven't talked to anybody but you about what happened yesterday. So you see, *mystery* doesn't apply here, not anymore."

"I disagree." Ben shook his head. "I may know some, but not nearly enough. I want to know so much more about you, Ivy."

A heavy sigh escaped from Ivy as her shoulders slumped. "Ben, I thought we agreed we could only be friends. I couldn't stand any more drama in my life right now."

Ben mentally berated himself for pushing. *Slow down,* his mind ordered. *Don't chase her away.* "You're right, of course. I won't push you, I promise. My guess is you need a friend right now a whole lot more than anything else."

A relieved smile lit Ivy's cocoa-colored face. "Thanks for understanding."

By then the band had finished and a swell of applause rose from the audience.

"They were great," Ivy enthused.

"Yeah, they were," Ben agreed. "But I have to admit I'm a little surprised that you like reggae music. It's an acquired taste . . . not everyone can appreciate the groove."

"For your information, Mr. Stephens, I happen to love reggae music. It's impossible to be depressed when you listen to reggae. It's uplifting and infectious and meant to be danced to."

Ben cocked his head, a mischievous smile playing about his lips. "Well, since you feel that strongly about it, there's a reggae club on Clark Street, just down the block from the stadium that I would love to take you to."

At her look of slight reproach, he quickly added, "Just as friends, of course."

Ivy's face softened. "We'll see." She turned in the direction of the park exit. "Would it be all right with you if we left now? I've been feeling a little sick to my stomach for a couple of days now . . . I'm sure it's just stress, but all these different food smells are not helping one bit."

Instantly, concern sprang onto Ben's face. "Are you OK? Of course we can leave; I'm really sorry you're not feeling well."

"No, I'm the one who's sorry for making you leave early. You didn't even get to use all your tickets."

Ben looked down at the strips of food tickets in his hand. "Don't worry about that. I can use these another day . . . the Taste will be going on all month. Come on, let's get you home."

"You are almost too good to be true, Benjamin J. Stephens." Ivy shook her head. "How did I get lucky enough to run into you?"

Ben shrugged. "I believe everything happens for a reason. And I also believe it's best not to question that reason. Sometimes, you just gotta go with the flow."

Ivy nodded. "Wise and kind. Yep, too good to be true."

This time Ben laughed. "All a part of the service, ma'am." He held out his hand. "Let's go."

"Did you ring the bell?"

Kim turned from the intercom panel embedded in the brick next to the door of Ivy's apartment building and gave Cherise a scathing look.

"Of course I rang the bell," Kim snapped. "She's not answering."

"But she must be here. There's her car." Danielle pointed out the late model Accord parked at the curb.

Trina shook her head. "She's so upset. That has to be why she's not answering. She must think we're here to dump on her or something."

"Why would she think that?" Danielle demanded. "We're her friends. She has to know we're here to help her."

"What makes you think she knows we're here at all?" Kim stepped down from the top of the stoop.

"She's not responding to the bell. Maybe she went for a walk or something."

"I just can't imagine that," Cherise said. "I'm telling you, she's inside hiding out, too embarrassed to let us in."

"Cherise, I don't know why you're so quick to assume something's wrong, or that Ivy must be embarrassed," Kim said. "You're assuming she thinks she made some kind of mistake or did something wrong. Maybe she's not feeling that way at all. Maybe she's feeling relieved."

Cherise snorted at that. "Relieved? About what? Keith was one of the finest men in town, not to mention one of the most successful. He's well on his way to becoming a vice president of that bank he works at, and—oh, yeah—did I mention he's *fine?* Why would she be *relieved* about giving all that up?"

"Ivy's a smart, level-headed woman. She would not have bolted from that church unless she had a damned good reason." Trina jumped to the defense. "So let's just all settle down and wait until we talk to Ivy before we make any judgments."

Cherise opened her mouth to respond, but Danielle raised a silencing hand.

"Look, there down the block. Is that Ivy coming this way?" Danielle squinted against the sun to try and make out the details of the approaching pair. "And could that be a damned good reason walking next to her?" A wicked grin appeared on Danielle's face.

All conversation ceased as the quartet of friends watched Ivy and Ben approach.

"Oh, great," Ivy muttered once she recognized her friends. She slowed her stride, assessing the situation.

"What is it?" Ben asked, slowing to match her pace.

"See those women on the steps of my building?" She nodded her head in their direction. "They're my bridesmaids . . . I mean, they would have been my bridesmaids . . . well, you know what I mean. Anyway, I'm sure they're here to check up on me. This is not good."

"What's not good?" Ben looked confused. "That your friends wanted to check on you?"

"No, that they've seen me with you," Ivy answered. "They're gonna have all kinds of questions about you and what I'm doing with you, and I'm not feeling it right now." Ivy's mouth set in a determined line. "Why don't you go on and leave? I'll handle this."

"I don't think that's such a good idea," Ben protested. "If I just leave without even speaking to them, it'll look like we've got something to hide— and we don't." Ben smiled at her. "Just friends, remember?"

Ivy nodded. "You're right—just friends." She squared her shoulders and strode toward the gauntlet of bridesmaids.

"Hey guys," Ivy called. She stopped at the end of the sidewalk in front of her building. "What y'all doing here?"

For an electric moment, none of the women spoke. Then, the dam broke and they all spoke at once.

"What are we doing here?" Cherise sounded incredulous.

"Checking on you," Trina said.

"Where have you been?" Kim demanded.

"So, who's your friend?" Danielle cast a sideways look at Ben.

"Whoa!" Ivy laughed. "Slow down, everybody. One at a time!" She reached for Ben's arm and guided him forward. "First of all, this is Ben Stephens. Ben, these are my best friends in the whole world, Kim, Trina, Cherise, and Danielle."

"Hello, ladies," Ben said cheerfully with a wave. "Beautiful day, isn't it?"

"Yes, lovely," Danielle managed to respond. The others only stood and stared at Ben as if he were some kind of alien invader. A long, tense moment passed as the women studied Ben and Ivy.

Ben cleared his throat, breaking the silence. "Well, uh, I guess I should be going now." He turned to Ivy and took her hand. "Thank you for accompanying me today. I hope you feel better soon."

Ivy returned the smile. "I'm going to be fine. Don't worry about me. And thank you for rescuing me again today." She squeezed the hand that still held hers. "That's getting to be quite a habit for you, Benjamin J. Stephens."

"All a part of the service, ma'am." Their eyes locked and a wave of intensely private energy passed between them. They stood that way, a split second longer than propriety dictated, before Ivy pulled both her eyes and her hand away from his hold.

Ben turned to face the intense scrutiny of Ivy's friends. "It was nice to meet you, ladies. Perhaps we'll see each other again." A megawatt smile lit his honey-colored face as he spun on his heels and walked away from Ivy's building.

Ivy retrieved her keys from her purse and opened the security door. The four would-be bridesmaids' heads turned from Ben's retreating back to Ivy, unabashed curiosity branded on their faces.

"OK, girlfriend." Kim broke the stunned silence. "What gives?"

"Can we have this conversation upstairs rather than here on the stoop?" Ivy held the door open for them to enter.

The women filed in through the door.

"Oh, we're gonna have a conversation, all right," Danielle muttered as she passed.

Ivy took a deep, bracing breath as her friends mounted the stairs to her apartment. *Well,* she thought. *Here goes nothing. . . .*

Seven

The phone was ringing when Ben entered his apartment.

"Bennie?"

Ben checked his watch and groaned inwardly. *I've done it now!*

"Hi, Momma. How are you today?"

"Bennie, we missed you this morning." The voice was slightly accusing.

"Sorry, Momma. I should have called, but something came up this morning and I couldn't make it." Ben smiled, images of Ivy in the park filling his mind. "How was breakfast?"

Sunday breakfast at the Stephens' home was a command performance. Judy Stephens absolutely insisted that her family make time every Sunday morning to share a meal and the news of their lives. Even as adults, Ben and his sisters, Dionne and Tracy, all knew that regardless of whatever else was going on in their lives, come Sunday morning, they had to go home.

"Breakfast was fine," Judy said impatiently, "but we were all waiting to find out if you heard anything about the fellowship."

The fellowship? Ben paused for a moment, sur-

prised at the fact that the pending fellowship
hadn't crossed his mind since . . . well, since Ivy
had burst into his life.

"No, ma'am, I haven't heard anything yet, but
the board did say it might take a few weeks to get
an answer."

"I don't know if that's good news or bad news,"
Judy huffed. "You know I'm so proud of you, Bennie, but I don't know how I feel about the prospect
of you spending six weeks in the African bush."

"Momma, now don't start. We've been through
all this, and if the fellowship is approved we'll go
through it all again. It's an amazing opportunity
to see the world, do what I love to do—teach, and
make some extra money for the summer."

"So you say, Bennie, so you say." Judy sounded
skeptical. "But I can't act like I'm excited about
you being so far away for so long."

"Think of it as an adventure, Momma," Ben insisted. "And I will be back in time for the start of
the school year in the fall. If I even get the fellowship, that is."

"Oh, you'll get it," Judy said confidently. "You
are a good person, and good things happen to
good people."

"Thanks, Momma," Ben smiled, "for that un-
biased opinion."

"By the way, Bennie, you never did say—why did
you miss breakfast this morning?"

Ben hesitated, not sure how to explain his ab-
sence. He had no doubt that if his mother or his
sisters knew the whole story about Ivy, they would
immediately condemn her for running out on her

wedding. For reasons he could not begin to put into words, he wanted to protect both his new friend and their new friendship from the judgment of his family. But lying to his mother was out of the question, so after a few moments of intense consideration, Ben decided on half an answer.

"I had to help out a friend this morning. It just took longer than I expected, and I should have called. I'm really sorry, Mamma. It won't happen again."

"A friend? Wouldn't happen to be a lady friend, would it?" Judy drew in a quick breath. "Tell me you didn't blow off your family for a woman."

Can't slide nothing past Momma. Ben shook his head. "It's not what you think. She's just a friend. And I didn't blow off my family." Ben took off his glasses and rubbed the bridge of his nose. "Tell you what. Let me make it up to you. I've got some food tickets for the Taste. What say I come and pick up you and Pops and we go to the park for lunch?"

For a long moment, Judy didn't answer. Ben feared he was in deeper trouble than an afternoon at the Taste of Chicago could rescue him from. Finally, she responded.

"That would be very nice, Bennie. I'll check with your father and make sure he's available."

Ben nodded, relieved. "I'll be by to pick you up within an hour." They finalized their plans and ended the conversation.

Ben crossed his apartment to pick up a packet of information from his kitchen table. Even though he knew the materials by heart, he pulled the papers out of their envelope and studied them yet again.

"Mr. Stephens, in recognition of your outstanding teaching ability and commitment to educational enrichment, the board of directors of the Julian Foundation invites you to apply for an international teaching fellowship."

Ben flipped through the papers, his decision to apply reaffirmed by the descriptions of the position and the work involved. When the opportunity was presented, Ben's first reaction was unbridled enthusiasm. He loved teaching high school—working with students and witnessing the moment when they "got it" was a joy for him. Typically, he taught summer classes, both for the joy of teaching as well as for the extra money he made. Even though he loved teaching, there was no chance he would get rich doing it. But this summer, he had not signed on to teach classes in Chicago, keeping his schedule clear in hopes of getting the Julian Fellowship.

Western Africa, he thought. *I'll spend six weeks teaching to and living with the Liberian people. This would be a great chance to see the world, make a difference in students' lives, and all the while get paid.*

Ben put the information packet back on the table and walked over to the living room window. Pushing the curtain aside, he stared out at his neighborhood, looking at everything but seeing nothing. His mind was in a whirl, thoughts warring for prominence.

For weeks, ever since I got the invitation to apply, the fellowship has been all I've thought about. Now all of a sudden, it hasn't crossed my mind once—not since I met

Ivy. Ben frowned. *Actually, my life has been royally disrupted ever since I met Ivy. I pissed off my best friend yesterday, and stood up my family today. What is it about that woman that has me acting so strange?*

He let the curtain drop back into place and moved away from the window. "I can't get involved with her," he said, his voice filling the empty apartment. "There are a million reasons why that's a bad idea."

But even as the sound of his voice filled his ears, Ben's thoughts drifted back to Ivy. *I wonder how she's doing with the bridesmaid posse. . . .*

"First of all, let me say that I'm sorry I haven't called anybody," Ivy began. She closed the door behind her and leaned back against it. Looking around the living room, she made eye contact with each of her friends. "I just wasn't ready to talk about it."

"With us—you mean you weren't ready to talk about it with us." Danielle cocked a brow. "Because you certainly seemed ready to talk about it with . . . Ben, was it?"

Ivy grimaced. "Whatever you're thinking about Ben and me, you're wrong. We're just friends. I just met him yesterday, in fact."

"Do tell." Kim crossed her arms and leaned back into the sofa.

"When I left the church yesterday, all I could think of was getting away. The closest thing I could find was the El train station. So I tried to get on the train, but my dress got caught in the door. Ben helped me get free." An almost imperceptible smile crossed Ivy's face as she caught the double meaning in the word "free."

"That's very interesting, but I think we're getting a little ahead of ourselves." Cherise sat at the dinette table, fiddling idly with one of the many unopened congratulation cards addressed to Mr. and Mrs. Keith Jamison. "*Why* did you leave the church yesterday? What happened? I thought you were excited about getting married."

Ivy paused, taking a deep breath to give her time to organize her thoughts. "I realized yesterday that I don't love Keith. Not the way a wife should love her husband. It suddenly dawned on me that I was making a lifetime commitment to the wrong man."

"So what are you saying—that this Ben is the right man?" Danielle stood next to Cherise.

"It doesn't have anything to do with Ben," Ivy said, exasperated. "I didn't even meet Ben until after I'd left the church. Ben is just a nice guy who was trying to help me out. This is about me . . . and my feelings, or lack of feelings, for Keith."

"I don't understand, Ivy. You seemed so happy." Trina's face was a study of confusion and hurt. "We've all been planning this wedding for months . . . having showers and parties and luncheons, going shopping for dresses and shoes . . . and never once did you say anything or even hint that this wasn't what you wanted."

"I know." Ivy shook her head sadly. "I guess I was caught up in the whirlwind. It was all so much fun . . . I was the center of attention, and we were all spending more time together than we had in years. There were so many details and so much to do, that I guess I never stepped back and looked at the big picture." Her voice trailed off for a moment as Ben's words filled her mind. "But I've come to realize that everybody wanting me to have a wedding has nothing to do with me wanting to have a marriage. I couldn't go through with being a wife just because everybody wanted me to be a bride."

The room fell quiet as the weight of Ivy's words settled around them. Ivy wiped away the tears that formed in the corners of her eyes.

Finally Kim broke the silence. "I had no idea you felt that way."

Ivy shrugged. "How could you? I didn't realize it myself until yesterday."

Cherise tossed the envelope in her hand back onto the pile in the center of the dinette table. "I guess I understand what you're saying. And if that's how you feel, you were right not to marry him. But Ivy, the way you handled it was still very messed up. You couldn't have found a more humane way to tell Keith?" Cherise shook her head slowly, a pitying look on her face. "You didn't see him in the church after you left. He was devastated."

Danielle nodded her agreement. "It was a hard thing to see—big, bad Keith Jamison looking like a deer caught in headlights. He was hurt and embarrassed." Danielle gave Ivy a piercing look. "Maybe leaving the church was best for you, but it sure wasn't best for Keith."

Ivy pushed away from the door and crossed the

room to stand in front of Danielle. "Don't you think I know that? Don't you think that was the hardest part for me? But do you think I'd be doing Keith any favors if I married him just because I didn't want to embarrass him?"

Danielle nodded slowly. "OK, I see your point."

"Have you talked to him?" Kim asked.

"Yesterday. He came here and I tried to explain." Ivy deliberately left out Ben's involvement in the previous day's activities.

"How did that go?" Cherise asked.

"About as well as it could. He didn't understand, and he was still very hurt and confused. I'm hoping after he's had a chance to process it all, he'll come to accept it."

"What about your parents?" Trina asked. "Your mom was pretty upset."

Ivy heaved a sigh. "Talking to them was almost as hard as talking to Keith. And talking to you guys hasn't been a picnic, either." A weary smile lit her face. "And now I'm tired of talking about the non-wedding. Can we let it go?"

Nodding, Kim stood and clapped her hands once. "Yes, we can. I'm pulling rank. As non-maid of honor, I declare this discussion closed. We came over here to see if Ivy was OK, and it seems that she is. Now let's see what we can do to help her get back to normal." Kim walked over to the wedding gifts piled in the corner. "What are you going to do with these?"

Ivy shrugged. "I haven't even begun to think about that yet. I guess I'll send them back."

Kim nodded. "OK, we can help organize that.

Trina, let's start checking these cards to see who sent what. Danielle and Cherise, you guys get the guest list and start finding addresses so we can return these gifts."

The women murmured their agreement and went to tend to their assigned duties. The tears that had been threatening in Ivy's eyes finally spilled over as she watched her friends come to her aid.

"You guys are the best . . . I love you so much." She lowered her head and wiped her eyes with her knuckles. "Thank you for understanding. And thank you for being here for me."

"Hey," Danielle said, "what're friends for?"

Smiling through her tears, Ivy hugged each of her friends. When the hugs were finished, she reached for one of the stacked packages gaily wrapped in silver wedding paper. She checked the card to see who sent the gift.

"Damn," she swore softly.

"What's wrong?" Trina turned to face her.

"This gift—it's from Keith parents." Ivy held the package out for inspection. "I guess I'm going to have to explain myself one more time. Mr. and Mrs. Jamison deserve to hear it from me—they had to be as embarrassed and upset as my parents were." Ivy handed the wedding gift to Trina. "I'm going to call them now. Wish me luck."

"You know we've always got your back," Kim reassured her.

Ivy smiled her thanks and went into the kitchen to make her call. As she dialed, she tried to plan what she would say to her almost in-laws. *I can only imagine what they must think of me. How can I possibly make them understand?*

Before Ivy was ready, Pat Jamison answered the phone.

"Hello?"

"Uh, hi Mrs. Jamison. It's Ivy."

The line hummed for a long moment. "Hello, Ivy. I must say, I'm surprised to hear from you."

"Yes, ma'am, I expect you would be after what happened yesterday."

"Well, yes, but that's not what I meant. I didn't think you'd be in town."

A pained expression scrunched Ivy's face. "You thought I ran off and left town? I guess I deserved that—"

"No, no, Ivy—listen. I thought you'd gone with Keith." Pat's voice revealed her confusion.

"Gone with Keith?" Now it was Ivy's turn to be confused. "What do you mean?"

"Keith left this morning to go to Maui—on your honeymoon. When he called to say he was going, I had hoped that meant you two reconciled and you were both going. I had no idea he would be going alone."

Ivy was momentarily stunned into silence. It took her several moments to process that bit of information. "No, ma'am," she managed finally. "We didn't reconcile." She shook her head as if Pat could see her. "The reason I'm calling is because I wanted to try and explain about yesterday."

"I don't know what you could say that would explain," Pat said. "But to be quite honest, it's not me or my husband to whom you owe an explanation. You need to explain yourself to Keith."

"I tried to yesterday after—" Ivy cut off the thought. "When I saw him."

"Well, apparently you weren't very convincing, because when I talked to my son this morning, I got the clear impression that he expected you two to work it all out. That's why I thought you had gone to Maui."

"I'll talk to Keith again when he returns." Ivy squared her shoulders. "But right now, I really want to talk to you. I want to apologize for the way I handled things yesterday."

"I'm not interested in your apologies, Ivy." Pat's words were more terse than her tone. "You square things with Keith, and you've squared things with me. The only thing that matters to me here is my son's happiness. So making amends to me is not what you need to do." Pat hung up then, not with an angry slam, just a definitive click that indicated she had said all she intended to say.

Ivy slowly returned the receiver to its hook. *Keith went to Maui.* She turned that notion over in her head a few times. Finally, she decided that was a good thing. *Maybe when he gets back, he'll be ready to accept my decision. Maybe he'll even meet someone in Hawaii who can help him get over it.*

"Ivy?" Cherise stood in the doorway to the kitchen, watching the play of emotions on Ivy's face. "Is everything all right?"

Ivy's head snapped up as if she had awakened from a trance. "Yes," she said firmly. "Everything is going to be just fine." She shook her head to clear her thoughts and took a step toward Cherise. "Where are we with the gift returns?"

Eight

"So who is she?"

Ben struggled to consciousness, having been jarred out of sleep by the shrill ring of his telephone. He barely remembered picking up the receiver, and suddenly the voice of his sister was barking out questions in his ear.

"Mmm?" was the best response he could manage.

"Bennie! Wake up!" It was Dionne, his older sister. "I know you're out of school for the summer, but still, you should be up and running by now."

"Whaddya want, Dee?" Ben grumbled.

"I want to know who this woman is who had you missing breakfast yesterday." Dionne made a tsking sound in her throat. "Momma told me that was your excuse."

Ben heaved a deep sigh and shook off the last vestiges of sleep. "Dee, this could have waited until later in the day. I am on vacation, you know."

"It's Monday morning, Bennie," Dionne chuckled wickedly. "If I have to be up, I figure everybody ought to be up. Now tell me what's going on."

"Nothing's going on, Dee. A friend of mine was in some trouble, and I had to help her out."

"Ben to the rescue, huh? It had to be some kinda trouble to make you miss breakfast. So you still haven't said—who is she?"

"You don't know her. Let it go, Dee." Ben sat up in bed and stretched, the phone cradled between his cheek and his shoulder. "So how're the kids?"

"Don't you go changing the subject on me, Benjamin Stephens." Dionne's tone was firm. "I want to hear about this woman."

Ben sat quietly for a long moment, considering how to deflect his persistent sister. *What can I tell her? What is there to say about Ivy?* In his mind's eye, images of the many faces of Ivy flashed past. He saw the distressed Ivy, in her damaged wedding gown. He saw the defensive Ivy, her back stiff, ready to face first the jilted groom and then her would-be bridesmaids. And he saw the relaxed Ivy, enjoying a rule-breaking slice of cheesecake. Ben felt a smile spread across his face. *What is there to say about Ivy, indeed.*

"Bennie? Are you still there?" Dionne's query broke into his thoughts.

"Yeah, Dee. I'm here." Ben refocused on his sister. "There is nothing I can tell you about *this woman* except she is my friend, and she needed some help."

"Uh-huh. . . ." Dionne didn't sound appeased. "I thought you decided you weren't going to get involved with anyone, since you'll likely be gone for the whole summer with that teaching fellowship."

Ben's brow furrowed. "Get involved? Slow down,

Dee. I just said I helped her out. I didn't say anything about getting involved."

"I know what you said . . . and I know what you didn't say." Dionne paused. "And I know what you won't say."

"Oh, is that right?" Ben snorted. "Tell you what, Dee—why don't you go back to work, and leave the psychic readings to the experts?"

"You can't fool me, Bennie. You never have been able to, ever since we were kids."

"Nobody's trying to fool you, Dee." Ben's patience was wearing thin. "Let it go. And speaking of *go*, I'm gonna get up from here and get my day started . . . since a certain sister of mine has seen to it I won't be sleeping in today."

"OK, Bennie. I have to say it—you sound awful defensive for a man with nothing to hide." The smile in Dionne's words seeped through the phone lines. "I'll talk to you later . . . count on it."

"Bye, Dee." Ben hung up the phone with no further comment. He flung the blanket aside and climbed out of bed. Crossing the floor heading to the bathroom, Ben shook his head vigorously as if trying to scatter unacceptable thoughts.

Involved? That's just ridiculous. Ben mentally ticked off the reasons again why getting involved with Ivy was a bad idea. And again, the list was only partially successful. Because what kept penetrating his mind, with much more force than a list of obstacles, were thoughts about Ivy and how she was holding up.

"That run-in with her bridesmaids probably wasn't any fun. I could just check on her," he muttered to the reflection in the bathroom mirror. *But I don't have her phone number.* The thought flashed across his mind. He considered his reflection for a moment. Finally he shrugged. "Well," he said, "I guess I'm going to have to stop by her apartment." He reached for a nearby washcloth and bar of soap. "Just to check," he muttered as he turned on the shower.

A small voice in his head made a derisive sound. *Right, who're you trying to convince?*

Ben stepped under the steamy running water, effectively drowning out the voice.

The morning found Ivy with much more time on her hands than she ever expected. After all, if things had gone as planned, she would have been in Hawaii celebrating her marriage. She and her friends had finished preparing the gifts for returns. The women had taken most of the gifts with them when they left the previous day, planning to return the presents to Chicago area guests. The only gifts that remained had come from out of town. Ivy's charge for the day was to arrange for a courier to pick up the boxes and ship them back to the senders. She was debating whether or not to include a note of explanation when her doorbell rang.

"Oh, what now?" Ivy's voice trailed off. She pushed the intercom button with great trepidation. "Yes?"

"Good morning, Ivy. It's Ben."

She shot a shocked looked at the intercom, as if the box was responsible for her surprise. *What is he doing here?* Unanticipated shivers shimmered through her as images of the handsome, steadfast Benjamin J. Stephens filled her mind. *Stop it, Ivy! Get a hold of yourself.* She took a deep breath and pushed the TALK button on the box.

"Ben? This is a surprise. What are you doing here."

"Just stopped by to check on you." Ben's voice filled her apartment. "When I left yesterday you were about to be interrogated by a bevy of bridesmaids. I just wanted to make sure you were OK."

Ivy smiled, warmed by his concern. "I'm fine, Ben. You really didn't have to come all the way over here for that."

"Well, I would have called, but I didn't have your number." Ben's response crackled through the intercom. "So I decided to drop by. Is this a bad time?"

Ivy hesitated, considering his question. *Is this a bad time?* She looked down at her pajamas, then over at the packages piled on the dinette table. *Actually, yes, it is a bad time,* her mind answered. *And it's a bad idea to keep letting this guy in—into your apartment and your life. Send him away; you don't need any more complications.*

But another voice, emanating from her chest, overruled. With a smile and a shrug, Ivy ignored the logical response and instead followed her heart.

"Benjamin J. Stephens, your timing is perfect." She pushed the button that would unlock the entry door. "Come on up."

When Ben entered Ivy's apartment, he was surprised to see that the majority of the wedding presents were gone. "What happened?" he asked, gesturing toward the now empty corner.

At first, Ivy furrowed her brow, but then she realized what he was asking. "My friends were terrific. They helped me return the presents yesterday. They took everything but the gifts from out of town. I've got to handle returning those."

"If you'd like, I could help you with that," Ben offered.

Smiling, Ivy shook her head in wonder. "You were a boy scout as a kid, weren't you?"

Ben chuckled. "I've been called that more than once."

"Of that I have no doubt. Is this what you do for a living? Aid damsels in distress?"

"Nah, I only rescue damsels part-time." Ben laughed again, a rich full sound that reverberated in Ivy's living room. "I teach high school. And since school is out for the summer, I have plenty of time for my *damsel aide* gig."

Ivy regarded him with new respect shining in her eyes. "You teach high school? In Chicago? You really are a hero."

Ben shook his head. "It's not that big a deal. And don't believe the hype—Chicago is filled with good kids who are working hard to get a good education. I'm just glad I can be a part of it. What about you? What do you do, normally?"

"I'm a corporate girl. I work in human resources at a huge accounting firm. Not nearly as rewarding as what you do, but it pays the bills." Ivy shrugged. "But for the next few days, I'm on my so-called honeymoon," she made a face, "so I don't want to think about work. If you were serious, I really could use your help returning these last few packages."

Ben doffed an imaginary hat. "At your service." He cocked his head at her. "But you might want to get dressed first."

Ivy looked down at her cotton pajamas, the shirt and pants decorated with fluffy white clouds against a pale-blue background. "You have a point. Be right back." She disappeared down the hall to change.

What are you doing? The voice exploded in Ben's mind. *You're involving yourself in this woman's life again! This is nothing but trouble!* Ben shook his head, trying to clear away the discouraging voice. "I'm only helping her return some packages," he mumbled under his breath. "I know what I'm doing." *Right . . . sure thing. . . .* The voice faded away.

In her bedroom, Ivy stood in front of the closet, struggling to decide what to wear. She pulled out a vibrant tropical print sundress that she had purchased expressly for Hawaii and held it up to her body.

"Might be a little much just to ship some packages," she muttered. She tossed the dress onto the bed and reached for another hanger. *Why am I having such a hard time deciding what to wear? Before Ben showed up, I would have thrown on a pair of jeans and a T-shirt and hit the road.* Ivy put her hands on her hips. "This is just silly," she declared. Slightly irritated at her own indecision, Ivy snatched a pair of black jeans from the closet and tossed them on the bed. She added a peach-colored shell blouse to the growing pile of clothes on the bed. Satisfied, she headed into her bathroom for her morning grooming.

We're just returning packages. She repeated the phrase in her mind over and over again. *It's nothing more than that. Ben's a nice guy, come to do a good deed. We're just returning packages. . . .*

Having almost convinced herself, Ivy quickly began to dress.

Keith Jamison sat at a poolside bar nursing a fruity tropical drink. Although he was dressed in traditional island vacation garb, sitting under a palm tree in full view of the Pacific Ocean, Keith did not fit the image of a laid-back vacationer. His hunched shoulders gave a clue to the turmoil churning his insides. His tightly clenched jaw revealed still more about the true nature of the man at the bar.

Ever since he had arrived on the island, Keith had been faced with reminders of his aborted wedding. It began when the hotel limousine showed up at the airport, fully stocked with champagne and pineapple for two. Ignoring the pitying looks from the hotel staff, ranging from everyone from the limo driver to the desk clerk, Keith had carried his own bags up to the suite—the honeymoon suite, to be exact—and encountered his and hers complimentary bathrobes, a basket of luscious tropical fruit, a romantic four-poster bed draped in sheer netting, and a balcony with an amazing view of the beach.

It was all as he had requested when he'd made the reservations—a perfect place to launch the perfect life. Now, it was all too much . . . too many reminders of his humiliation. Keith had spent most of his so-called vacation in the same spot—seated at the bar, a vacant look trained either on the depths of the ocean or the depths of his glass. A few women had approached him—even in his melancholy, Keith was still a stunningly handsome man—but he had tersely rebuffed their advances. By now, his fourth day in Hawaii, almost everyone at the resort, staff and guests, knew to steer clear of the "brutha with a 'tude."

She just ran out on me . . . on me! *Doesn't she know who I am?* His thoughts tortured him yet again. *Wonder if she's missing me yet? Wonder if she's sorry yet?* Keith twirled his swizzle stick around the drink, watching the tiny vortex that spun around in the glass. *I have to know what's going on,* he decided suddenly.

"Bartender! Is there a phone here I can use?"

The bartender, surprised by Keith's sudden outburst, recovered quickly and handed Keith a cordless phone.

"For an outside call, you have to dial eight, then enter either your calling card or room number," the bartender said.

"Yeah, thanks," Keith said, snatching the phone. He slid off the barstool that had come to be his and crossed the pool deck to a relatively isolated table next to a huge hibiscus bush. After punching in a seemingly endless series of numbers, the connection was made and Keith waited impatiently for his call to be answered.

"Hello?"

"Hi, it's me."

"Keith," the feminine voice registered pleased surprise. "I've been hoping to hear from you."

Keith ignored that remark. "What's going on? Have you seen Ivy?"

A heavy sigh met his question. "I can't believe you called me to ask about Ivy."

Keith shrugged. "Why else would I call you?"

The silence that followed drew out so long that Keith began to get anxious. Finally, the woman answered. "Why else, indeed?" She fell silent again, and Keith could imagine her struggling to control her anger. "Well, since you asked," she continued, "I did see Ivy the day after the would-be wedding. She was fine. As a matter of fact," the woman paused dramatically, "she wasn't alone when I saw her. She was with a man named Ben. She said he was a friend . . . anybody you know?"

"Ben?" At first, Keith couldn't place the name. Then it clicked into place. "Ben! Was he light-skinned, skinny, wearing glasses?"

The woman laughed. "He most certainly was not skinny. I would describe him as honey-brown, well-toned, with expensive-looking gold frames that complemented his intensely expressive eyes." She chuckled again. "I guess it's all just a matter of perspective. You never did say—is he anybody you know?" The question oozed sugar.

Keith gripped the phone so hard his hand began to ache. "He is nobody," Keith ground out through clenched teeth. "He is nothing. He does not matter."

"If you say so," the woman replied sweetly. "How is Hawaii? You miss me?"

Keith grimaced. "Hawaii," he muttered, more to himself than to her, "is too far away." He drummed his fingertips on the table, strategizing.

"Keith? Are you still there? Did you say something?"

The questions roused him from his contemplation. "Never mind. Thanks for the info. Talk to you later." He disconnected the line with no further conversation.

Ben, eh? Guess Miss Ivy is not missing me as much as I had hoped. After a few moments of deep thought, Keith pushed the TALK button on the cordless phone and connected with the hotel front desk. "I need to get on the next flight back to Chicago. I've got some business to attend to."

Nine

"It's just a movie," Ben insisted. "And maybe lunch afterward. C'mon, Ivy . . . you've got some free time, I've got some free time—what's the problem?"

Ivy shook her head, fully aware that Ben could not see the movement through the phone. "The problem is that we've spent time together every day since my would-be wedding. The problem is I can't possibly even consider getting involved, Ben. I thought you understood that."

In the four days since they'd met, Ivy and Ben had either seen each other or talked on the phone each day. It started with Ben serving as her sounding board and weeping shoulder, but their connection was beginning to change subtly.

"I *do* understand," Ben shot back. "Who said anything about getting involved? I just want to see this movie, and I don't want to see it alone. All my friends are at work this time of the day. You're the only person I know with the daytime free."

"The only person you know?" Ivy said skeptically. "What about the other teachers at your school? They must all be on the same schedule as you."

"Some of them are. Most of them are teaching

summer school. And the ones that aren't are not people I'd want to spend an afternoon with. It's just a movie," Ben repeated. "And maybe lunch afterward. Is there some other reason you don't want to go? Something you're not telling me about?"

Ivy paused, trying to decide how to answer. How could she tell him that even if he understood that they couldn't get involved, she wasn't sure if her heart did? How could she admit that each moment she spent with him drew her closer and closer to falling for him? How could she face the fact that Benjamin J. Stephens was fast becoming much more than a friend?

It's just because I'm vulnerable right now, she rationalized. *After what I've been through, if any man showered this kind of attention on me, I would be feeling this way about him. I need to step back and get some perspective. I need to handle my life.*

"C'mon, Ivy. What do you say?" Ben's question broke into her thoughts. "You gonna make me go to this movie alone?"

It was in her rational mind to refuse. She formed the words in her mind and opened her mouth to let him down gently.

"Well, we can't have you going off to the movies by yourself. Anything could happen." The response surprised her as much as it seemed to surprise Ben.

"Excellent!" Ben enthused. "I'll pick you up around noon. And don't eat anything. We'll go to lunch after the movie."

"I said movie," Ivy declared. "I didn't say anything about lunch."

"True," Ben allowed, "but after the movie you'll be hungry, and I couldn't have that on my conscience. See you soon." Ben severed the connection before Ivy could lodge a further protest.

Ivy smiled in spite of herself. "Pretty sneaky, Stephens," she said out loud, then headed to her bathroom to shower.

Promptly at noon, Ivy's doorbell rang. Smiling, she went to press the intercom button.

"Right on time, Mr. Stephens?" her voice was teasing.

"As always, Miss Daniels." Ben's response filled her apartment. "Are you ready?"

"Just about." Ivy pushed the entry button. "Come on up." She unlocked her apartment door so Ben could walk in once he reached the top of the stairs. She then rushed back to her bedroom—presumably to finish getting ready, but in reality, on a feminine level of which she was not totally conscious, Ivy wanted to make a grand entrance. She took one last look in the mirror mounted above her dresser. She was wearing a multicolored headband that lifted the tiny twists of hair away from her face. Her rich cocoa complexion was smooth and makeup free. The only concession to vanity was the wine-tinted gloss that colored her lips. She cast a quick look downward, checking to make sure her jeans and T-shirt were ready for her entrance. When she'd chosen her look for the day, Ivy had made a conscious decision to avoid "date" clothes. She believed the jeans and casual T-shirt conveyed a message that this outing was no more significant than it would have been if her companion were one of her girlfriends. But even so, she had to be honest with herself and admit she'd chosen this particular T-shirt because the sleeves were cut high enough on her arm to bare the distinctive ivy vine tattoo. She smiled now, remembering Ben's initial reaction to her body art.

"Hello?" Ben's voice drifted down the hall. "Where'd everybody go?"

"Be right there," Ivy called in response. She took a deep breath, squared her shoulders, and headed out to greet him.

"Hi, Ben. Ready to go?" Ivy's smile lit her face.

Ben pulled his gold oval glasses down a bit and peered over the top of the frames. "You look great," he complemented. "There aren't many women who can make jeans and a T-shirt look elegant." He returned her smile as he looked her over carefully. "I haven't seen that in a while." He pointed to her tattoo. "It really is beautiful. Did it hurt much?"

Ivy laughed. "Not nearly as much as I expected it to. It wasn't pain-free, but the artist worked very quickly, so it wasn't so bad."

"I'm curious . . . what made you get a tattoo? I mean, you don't seem like a tattoo kind of girl."

"What kind of girl is that?"

"You know, a biker chick or mud wrestler, somebody tough like that."

She cocked her head at him. "That's a terrible stereotype," she chided. "I got a tattoo because I thought it would be a perfect expression of me." She flexed her arm, causing the outline of firm muscles to appear under her cocoa-colored skin. "I work hard to stay fit; I wanted a little permanent jewelry to show it off."

A slow grin spread across Ben's face. "I have to say, you made a good choice. Looks really hot." He met her eyes, and an intensely intimate charge passed between them. "The tattoo, I mean," he clarified. "The tattoo looks really hot."

Ivy inclined her head slightly. "Thanks."

The loud buzz from her intercom shattered the moment. Ivy's brow furrowed as she crossed the room to answer the call.

"Yes?"

"Ivy, it's me. Let me in."

Ivy backed away from the intercom, surprised horror etched on her face. Insistent buzzing pulled her back to the button.

"Mom? What are you doing here?"

"I wanted to check on you and bring you some food. I bet you haven't eaten a thing since Saturday. Buzz me up."

Ivy pressed the entry button as she spun to face Ben. "You have to hide!"

"What?" Ben's face scrunched in question. "Why?"

"Mom can't see you here—I'd never hear the end of it." Her panic was mounting. "Please, Ben—just go back into the bedroom until I can get rid of her."

"I don't understand. . . ."

"Ben! There's no time!" A quick knock-knock on the door confirmed Ivy's words. "It'll only be a couple of minutes, I promise." She gently pushed him toward the hallway.

Ben grudgingly conceded to her request, crossing the hallway in three long strides and slipping into her bedroom.

Ivy checked to make sure her visitor was hidden from sight, then opened the door to admit her mother.

"Hi, baby." Grace brushed a kiss on her daughter's cheek. "What took you so long?"

"I was back in my room getting dressed." Ivy stood in the doorway. "I wasn't expecting you. What brings you by?"

"I just wanted to check on you. We haven't spoken since Saturday . . . I was worried about you." Grace brushed past Ivy to place the casserole dish she was carrying on the dinette table. "I brought you some chicken and rice because I know you haven't eaten any real food—greasy fast food, if anything."

Ivy grimaced. "Thanks, Mom, but you really didn't have to do that. I'm doing just fine. As a matter of fact, I was just on my way out—so if you'll excuse me." Ivy turned and reached for the doorknob.

"You're going out?" Grace raised a delicately arched brow. "Where?"

"Just to the movies, and maybe lunch afterward."

"Oh." Grace packed a wealth of meaning in that one syllable. "Do you think that's a good idea?"

"Why not?" Ivy looked confused. "I'm just going to the movies."

"But what if someone sees you? Don't you think you ought to lay low for a while?"

"Huh? Why?"

"Well, darling, you created quite a spectacle when you ran out on the wedding. People are still talking about it—some of my friends have called to let me know they got their gifts back, so even people who weren't there now know what happened." Grace folded her arms across her body. "Seems to me you really ought to stay out of sight until the furor dies down. Out of respect, if nothing else."

Ivy's mind reeled. "Out of respect? Mom, nobody died. You're being a little dramatic, aren't you?"

"No, Ivy, I'm not! You're right, nobody died, but the whole affair was terribly embarrassing. You need to give people time to forget before you go out acting like nothing even happened. You decided not to marry Keith. Fine, I can accept that, but I think it's wrong for you to be out flaunting that decision." Grace made a harumphing sound in her throat. "Gallivanting around town a mere four days after you jilted your groom—really, Ivy."

Ivy's hand fell away from the doorknob as she turned away from her mother's searing gaze. Dark feelings of guilt and shame rose up from her core, coloring her thoughts.

"Mom, I know Saturday was embarrassing—it was for me, too—but I had to do it. I don't love Keith." Ivy forced herself to meet Grace's eyes. "I'm sorry if this has been difficult for you. That wasn't what I wanted. But I couldn't go through with the wedding just to spare you some embarrassment in front of your friends."

"Ivy, I have already said I accept that decision. I still think you made the wrong choice—Keith is a wonderful man—but I have accepted it. I'm not talking about the wedding anymore. I'm talking about how you carry yourself now. It's too soon for you to be out acting as if things were back to normal." Grace paused as a thought hit her. "Movies and lunch? That sounds like a date." She rolled her eyes dramatically. "Oh, Lord, please tell me you are not going on a date!"

"It's not a date, Mom." Ivy hung her head. "I just wanted to get out of here for a while."

"Well, you have to make your own decisions. You always do." Grace pointedly glared at Ivy's tattoo as she prepared to leave. "But I would be derelict in my duties as your mother if I didn't tell you I think you're making a mistake—again."

Ivy had no reply; her deflated posture was response enough. Grace held out her arms and walked over to hug her daughter. Neither resisting nor yielding, Ivy allowed herself to be wrapped in Grace's arms.

"You know I love you, baby," Grace whispered in Ivy's ear. "I only want what's best for you." Grace released Ivy and opened the door. "Call me later?"

Ivy nodded and murmured something that could have been agreement. Grace reached out and stroked Ivy's cheek. "It's going to be OK . . . just give it a little time." Grace left then, pulling the door closed tightly behind her.

Ivy leaned into the door, resting her forehead against the hard surface, emotionally drained from the visit. After a few silent moments, Ben emerged from the bedroom.

"I heard most of that. Are you OK?"

"I'm fine," she said quietly. "And if you heard, then you'll understand when I say I can't go with you today."

Ben shook his head. "No, I don't understand. Look, Ivy, I'm not one to talk about anybody's mother, but yours was dead wrong."

Ivy turned to face him, a defensive look etched on her face. "Mom loves me," she said. "She has my best interests at heart."

"I don't doubt that," Ben agreed. "But she's wrong if she wants you to hide out like you've committed some kind of crime. Ivy, we've been through all this—you did the right thing."

"That's not the issue," Ivy said flatly. "Yes, I did the right thing, but I did it the wrong way. And now I need to give everyone time to get over it."

Ben snorted at that. "People getting over it is their problem, not yours. Why should you have to lay low until the gossip dies down? I say go out and face it head-on, with your head held high." Ben took her limp hand and enclosed it between his. Rubbing gently, he tried to soothe her frayed nerves. "Your mom was right about one thing: it will be OK in time. But you need to go on and live your life. How people react to that is their problem, not yours." He bent slightly and cocked his head until his eyes met hers. "Please go out with me."

Ivy stood for a moment, locked in the power of his earnest gaze, her resistance weakening with each warm stroke on her hand. Her sense of obligation and propriety warred with her desire for fun and escape. Finally, she pulled her hand away from him.

"I can't."

"Why?" Ben prodded.

"It just wouldn't be right. If someone were to see me with you . . ." Her voice trailed off as she shook her head.

"Ivy, Chicago is a huge city! It's not like we're in Mayberry going downtown to the movin' picture show." Ben smiled encouragingly. "What are the chances somebody you know is going to see us?"

Ivy paused, considering the logic of his words. "I guess you haven't heard of Murphy's Law. You know, anything that can go wrong, will?"

Ben laughed. "I've heard of it. But I'm a proponent of Stephens's Law: This above all, to thine own self be true."

Ivy's brow furrowed. "Isn't that Shakespeare?"

"Busted!" Ben chuckled. "But Shakespeare, Stephens—does it really matter who said it? It's still true."

A pensive silence stretched between them as Ivy considered her options. "OK," she said finally. "I'll go." Ben whooped his approval. "But only to the movies," she continued. "I don't think I'm ready to risk being seen in a restaurant with a man—even a man who is just my friend."

Ben shrugged. "I guess a movie is better than

nothing. I still say if anybody has a problem, that's their issue, not yours."

"I hear you, Ben. But I have to do this my way." Ivy beamed with the first genuine smile that appeared on her face since her mother had buzzed the intercom. "Let me get my purse, and I'll be ready to go."

Moments later, Ivy and Ben climbed into his car and headed to a movie theater in a suburb far west of Ivy's apartment.

"Please remain buckled in your seat until the aircraft has come to a complete stop at the terminal and the captain has extinguished the fasten seat belt sign."

Keith ignored part of the flight attendant's instructions, releasing the buckle on his seat belt so he could be one of the first in the aisle to retrieve his carry-on bag from the overhead compartment.

Won't be long now, he thought. Once he decided to return to Chicago, Keith had been in constant motion. He'd booked a flight, checked out of the hotel, and caught a cab to the airport with only minutes to spare before takeoff. All during the long flight, Keith had been single-minded in his determination to right the wrong.

It's time for me to reclaim my woman—and my dignity. She's had long enough to think about what she's done.

The plane bumped to a halt, jarring Keith out of his reflections. He sprang from his seat and quickly got his bag. But all his haste was wasted when he found himself stuck midway in the aisle behind a family with three children who were obviously returning from their vacation in the sun.

Aw, c'mon, Keith's mind screamed. He took a deep breath and forced himself to be patient. *Ivy's not going anywhere. By now, she'll be relieved to see me. I'll forgive her the attack of cold feet, and we'll pick up and go on with our life together.*

A serenely confident smile spread across Keith's chiseled features. *It won't be long now. . . .*

"Oh, it was a ridiculous story line. All that movie had going for it was car crashes, explosions, gunfire, and bloodshed."

"What else does a movie need? I don't understand your complaint."

It was the tail end of a good-natured argument that had raged ever since Ben and Ivy left the movie theater.

"Let's see . . . a plot would have been nice," Ivy pretended to ponder the question. "And maybe a little character development. I would have liked to have cared about why that man was shooting anything that moved."

Laughing, Ben shrugged. "What does it possibly matter why he was shooting? Did you see those special effects? There's your plot."

Ivy shook her head with mock disgust. "Men," she muttered.

Ben eased his Mustang into a parking spot within a block of Ivy's apartment building. He chuckled as he set the brake. "I suppose next time you'll want us to go to one of those weepy chick flicks."

"At least those chick flicks, as you call them, have a developing plot and actually tell a story!" Ivy consciously ignored his reference to "next time." For Ivy, the future was too uncertain to plan any farther ahead than the next five minutes.

Ben's good humor stayed as he climbed out of his car and crossed to the passenger side to open Ivy's door. If he noted her lack of response to his comment, he gave no sign of it.

The pair started down the street toward Ivy's apartment, an easy banter bouncing back and forth between them. Ben saw him first.

"Not again," he grumbled.

"What?" Ivy stopped in her tracks, immediately sensing his change in mood.

"Don't look now, but I think you've got company." Ben nodded at a point several feet down the street. Ivy's eyes followed his gesture, and she gave a small gasp once she saw who had attracted Ben's attention.

"Keith," she breathed. "What is he doing here? I thought he was in Hawaii." Ben knew these were rhetorical questions, so he didn't attempt to offer a response. Even though he could feel his jaw muscles tense up and his first urge was to leap to Ivy's defense or put her back in the car and drive away, Ben decided to follow her lead.

Keith was standing in the middle of the sidewalk, his fists balled and resting on his trim hips. Anger, disgust, or disappointment—Ivy couldn't decide which—colored his face. *Looks like Mom was right,* she thought. *I should have just stayed home and out of sight.*

"Murphy's Law in full effect," she murmured. Hesitantly at first, then with more confidence, Ivy walked up to her ex-fiancé. Ben followed, staying a few respectful feet behind her. She stopped in front of Keith, pausing for a moment to fully assess him.

No matter what else I feel or don't feel for him, there's no denying he is one fine brother. The thought flashed in her mind.

"Hi. Nice tan."

Keith gave a dry, humorless chuckle. "The weather in Hawaii is beautiful this time of the year. You should have been there."

Ivy chose to let that remark drop. "You're back early. Wasn't the trip booked for a week?"

"Turns out a solo honeymoon is not all it's cracked up to be," Keith said. "I got lonely, so I decided to cut the trip short." He looked past her, casting a searing stare at Ben. "I can see that you managed to ward off the loneliness, though." He turned his gaze back to Ivy. "Why is *he* here again?"

"Ben is my friend," Ivy said, feeling defensive. "He's been helping me through a difficult time."

"A difficult time," Keith repeated. "It didn't have to be a difficult time, Ivy. This was supposed to be the best time of our lives. But you ran out on our wedding, and told me you were not ready." Keith gestured angrily at Ben, who was standing a few feet behind Ivy. "And for the second time in less than a week I find you with this guy. I asked you once before, but I think it bears repeating: Is he the reason behind your unreadiness?"

"And I told you once before, Ben is just my friend. I can use all the friends I can get right about now, but that's all he is—a friend. What happened between you and me was just that—between you and me." Ivy folded her arms across her chest, standing her ground. "Why are you here, Keith? Haven't we said all we needed to say?"

"Not by a long shot." With barely contained fury, Keith stepped toward her. "I told you before I left Saturday that this is not over." He grabbed her hand. "Tell your friend to get lost so we can talk."

Before Ivy could respond, Ben was at her side. "Her *friend* isn't going anywhere. And you need to calm down before the situation gets out of control."

"You need to back up out my face before the little bit of control I do have snaps and I break your face," Keith snarled.

"Don't hold back." Ben's temper was rising to match Keith's. "Bring it on."

Keith dropped Ivy's hand and began to advance on Ben. Quickly, Ivy positioned herself between the men.

"This is beyond ridiculous! Both of you calm down right now! This is not going to solve anything."

"Tell your *friend* to back off," Keith replied, never taking his eyes off Ben. "I've had a long day, and I'm not feeling like putting up with any mess today."

Ben opened his mouth to respond, but Ivy raised a silencing hand.

"Go home, Keith," she said. "You need to relax and unwind. If you insist, we can talk later, but not now."

"Go home?" Keith was incredulous. "You're sending me away? What about him? You're telling me to go and not him?"

"Yes, Keith," Ivy said firmly. "I want you to go home. I think it's best for everybody." Ivy sensed the significance of the choice she was making, but in the heat of the moment, the full impact of her decision had not yet registered in her mind.

"Best for everybody?" Keith regarded her with astonishment, all the fight knocked out of him. Ben watched silently, relaxing his guard only slightly.

"Get in your car, Keith." Ivy gently pulled him in the direction of the BMW. "I've seen enough explosions and bloodshed for one day."

Keith looked down at her quizzically. "What?"

"Never mind," Ivy muttered. "Just go. We'll talk later if you want."

They had reached his car by then. Keith shot one last hate-filled look at Ben, then unlocked his car door. "I don't appreciate being treated like this, Ivy," he said in a low whisper. "I deserve better than being kicked to the curb like yesterday's trash. You were supposed to by my wife by now." Keith's tone grew plaintive. "I still don't understand what happened."

"I tried to explain it to you Saturday; I don't know what else I can say."

"Say you love me. Say you'll marry me. Say we

can put all this behind us and get on with our lives."

Ivy hesitated for a moment, trying to formulate her answer. "I will agree that we need to put this all behind us and get on with our lives. But we probably have very different interpretations of that statement."

"You know, I'm not going to beg you to come back to me forever. There are other options."

"I don't know what you mean by that, but understand that I don't want you to beg me—not now, not ever. I made a hard choice, Keith. It was painful for a lot of people, you most of all, and I'm sorry for that. But I stand by my decision."

"We'll see." Keith leaned over to kiss her. Ivy pulled back, so Keith redirected the kiss to her cheek. "We'll see," he repeated. He climbed into the car and gunned the engine. Ivy stepped onto the sidewalk and watched, shaking her head, as the squeal of Keith's tires accompanied his peal down the street.

"I feel like I should apologize to you." Ben approached her.

"Why?" Ivy turned to face him, the emotional drain of her confrontation with Keith causing her shoulders to slump. "You didn't start the fight."

"Yeah, but if I hadn't insisted you go to the movies with me, we would have never run into him."

Ivy shrugged. "If I hadn't gone to the movies, I'd have just been here when Keith first arrived. And I'd have had to face him just that much sooner."

"I still feel bad. I intended to get you away from

it all for a while." Ben shoved his hands in his pockets. "Seems like I just made it worse."

"My mom always says, the road to hell is paved with good intentions." Ivy gave a rueful chuckle. "Mom's two for two today." She shook her head as if trying to shake off upsetting thoughts. "I'm going to go on up now. Thanks for the movie."

"I wish I could believe you meant that," Ben said.

"I really do," she assured him. "I like hanging out with you, Ben. You're the only person in my life these days who isn't coming down on me, questioning my actions and decisions." She crossed the space between them and stroked her hand against his cheek. "Thanks again for being my friend."

Ben gripped handfuls of his pants pockets to restrain himself. The urge to pull her into his arms was nearly overpowering. *It's getting harder and harder just to be your friend. . . .* The words registered in his mind but he managed to stop himself before he spoke them aloud.

"Being your friend is my pleasure," he whispered as he nuzzled his cheek against her palm.

"I'd better go," Ivy said, suddenly timid as she pulled her hand away. "Call me later?"

"If you'd like."

"Yes," she nodded. "I'd like. Talk to you soon." She turned on her heel and headed up the steps to her building, while she still had the will to make the walk alone.

Ten

"Good morning, Bennie. I'm so glad we didn't have to send a search party out looking for you this week." The young woman stood in the doorway with her hands on her hips.

Ben made a face as he bent to kiss his sister's cheek. "Tracy, after all the commotion last Sunday, only death would make me miss breakfast this week."

Tracy smiled at her handsome older brother and stepped aside so he could enter their parents' house. The Stephens family home base was an attractive ranch-style home in the Chicago suburb of Harvey. Judy and Gregory Stephens had worked hard to provide a comfortable upbringing for their children, and the middle-class neighborhood had been the perfect setting. Now that both elder Stephenses were nearing retirement, they had much more time to devote to their favorite hobby—gardening. The grounds around the house were testimony to the meticulous care Judy put into her flowers and Gregory put into his lawn.

The Sunday morning breakfast tradition had started when the Stephens' brood were children, and had continued ever since. It was important to

Judy that her family stay close, and a relaxed Sunday breakfast had worked wonders toward achieving that goal. Even during the college years, when Ben and his sisters were away at school, Judy insisted on a long-distance conference call each Sunday morning. Now that each of the Stephens siblings had set up housekeeping in the area, Sunday breakfasts were back in full swing.

"Dee here already?" Ben looked past his sister into the house.

"Everybody's here and waiting for you, Bennie." Tracy motioned inside.

"I'm not late, am I?" Ben sounded worried.

"No, not yet," Tracy assured him. "But after what happened last week, Mom had decided if you didn't show up within the next ten minutes, she was driving into town to get you herself."

Ben rolled his eyes. "Sounds just like Momma. Well, you can call off the rescue squad; I'm here."

Tracy closed the door behind him and followed her brother into the dining room. "So, tell me about her."

Ben stopped and turned to face her. "Tell you about whom?" His eyes narrowed suspiciously.

"Don't try that with me—you know who." Tracy crossed her arms. "Whoever this woman was who had you missing breakfast last week. Momma and Dee told me it was because of a woman, but neither of them knew much more than that. So what gives, bro? You can tell me," she coaxed.

"Gimme a break, Trace. I'll tell you exactly the same thing I told Mom and Dee: she was a friend in trouble and I just wanted to help out. Now can we let it drop?" Ben's exasperation was apparent.

"Man, Dee was right. You are defensive about this woman." Tracy gave her brother a teasing smile. "I can't wait to get the whole story."

Shaking his head in frustration, Ben turned from his sister and entered the dining room where his family was gathering.

"Good morning, everybody." Ben crossed to the head of the table and dropped a kiss on the top of his father's balding head. "Something smells good. Waffles this morning, Momma?" he called into the kitchen.

Judy entered through a swinging door that connected the kitchen and dining room, laden with a large platter of steaming Belgian waffles. "Morning, Ben. You made it just in time . . . the waffles won't stay hot forever."

"Hi, Momma." Ben's tone had just the right amount of contrition. He reached for the platter in her hands. "These look delicious. Is that sausage I smell cooking?"

Dionne, the oldest Stephens sibling, emerged from the kitchen carrying a platter of sausage links. "Nice of you to come, Bennie," she teased. "I guess your friend is out of danger this week?"

"I tried to get him to tell me about her, but he's being very tight-lipped," Tracy said as she settled at her spot around the table.

"Now you girls stop teasing your brother," Greg Stephens defended his son. "I'm sure he had a very good reason for missing breakfast last week, and I'm sure if he wants to tell you about it, he will."

"Thanks, Dad." Ben smiled gratefully at his father. He set the platter of waffles in the center of the cherrywood dining table.

A sly grin appeared on Greg's face. "After all, every man is entitled to a secret now and then."

"Aw Dad, not you, too!" Ben hung his head in mock defeat. "You all are making a much bigger deal out of this than it is. I just helped a friend last week, it's as simple and as straightforward as that."

"A woman friend," Tracy said.

"Who caused you to miss breakfast," Dionne added.

"And you didn't bother to call to say you wouldn't be here," Judy made the final point.

"Look, I'm here now, and I'm hungry. Can the interrogation wait until after I've eaten?" Ben sat in his spot and reached for the orange juice pitcher.

"I agree with Ben," Greg said. "Waffles first—grilling later."

The Stephens women nodded their agreement, but Ben had no doubt that the subject was far from closed. Once everyone was seated at the customary places, Greg blessed the food, and the breakfast began in earnest.

"The kids at their father's house?" Ben asked Dionne.

Dionne nodded. "Yep, it's his weekend. They'll be home later this evening."

"How's that going?" Tracy asked.

"Well, the kids had a hard time during the divorce, but they seem to be dealing with it just fine now. They get to go to their dad's twice a month and eat all manner of junk food and stay up all night." Dionne's words had a trace of bitterness.

"Don't worry about the kids, Dee," Judy said. "Kids are pretty resilient; they'll be fine. On the other hand, you don't seem to be handling it very well."

"I really am, Mom," Dee assured her. "Walter and I divorced a long time ago, and even though it was painful, it had to happen. We were not destined for forever."

Ben chewed thoughtfully on a piece of waffle. Swallowing, he chose his words carefully. "If you had known then what you know now, would you still have gotten married?"

Dionne considered the question. "There is no easy answer to that. Divorce is ugly and painful under the best of circumstances, so to avoid that, yes, I would have not married him. But on the other hand, if I had never married Walter, I would not have those two great kids. So I guess I would still marry him, even if I knew then what I know now."

"But just because of the kids?" Ben persisted.

"Yes," Dionne said slowly. "If there weren't kids involved, that question would be a no-brainer. What's up with you, Ben? You've never asked me anything like this before."

"Nothing's up." Ben shrugged. "Just curious, I guess."

"Uh-huh," Dionne replied, unconvinced.

The breakfast topics turned to other things:

Tracy's new job, Judy's petunias, Greg's golf game.
Ben laughed and talked with his family, but part
of his mind was elsewhere—thinking about Ivy, to
be precise. He wondered if Dionne's own failed
marriage might make her an ally if the time ever
came to tell Ivy's story. *And why would that time
come?* A voice in his head demanded. *It would only
be necessary if you got involved with Ivy . . . and you
have already decided not to do that, right?*

Ben brushed his hand past his head as if shooing
a pesky insect, and turned his full focus on the
breakfast conversation. But not before one last re-
bellious thought crossed his mind. *I was just wondering . . .*

Ivy curled up on her sofa and burrowed her head
in the brightly patterned comforter she had
wrapped herself in—not so much to ward off a chill,
but rather to ward off the world. She had closeted
herself in the apartment ever since the sidewalk confrontation with Keith, screening her calls and ignoring the door buzzer. It was her last day of
self-imposed exile; the next day her "honeymoon"
vacation days were over, and she had to report back
to work.

The phone's insistent ring penetrated the flimsy
sound barrier the comforter provided. Ivy let her
answering machine get that call, just as she had
the numerous calls that had come before. She figured it was Keith again, and she still wasn't up to
dealing with him.

"Ivy? Pick up! I know you're there!" Keith's

voice filled her apartment, confirming her suspicion. "Look, just pick up so I'll know you're OK. This isn't like you . . . I'm worried. C'mon Ivy, please pick up."

Ivy started to reach for the phone, but pulled her hand back. The machine disconnected, ending the call. "Tomorrow is soon enough to face the world," she decided. Her eyes drifted over to the beautiful arrangement of spring flowers that spilled out of a clear glass vase on her coffee table. One of her neighbors had brought the flowers in and left them outside her door; Ivy had ignored the buzzer when the deliveryman came. Her eyes fell to the card lying on the table next to the vase.

"I'm sorry I was such a jerk yesterday. I still love you, please forgive me—K."

That made Ivy feel even worse. *Keith should not be apologizing to me,* she thought. *After all that's happened, an apology is the last thing I deserve.*

In the past few days, she had ignored not only Keith's calls, but calls from her mother and all her girlfriends. The one call she hadn't received was the only one she wanted, a call from Ben. It rattled her to realize how much and how quickly she had come to depend on Ben's quiet strength. A half-dozen times she had picked up the phone to call him, but then decided against it out of fear of sending him the wrong message.

Ben's a great guy; he doesn't deserve my baggage, she told herself over and over. *It wouldn't be fair to lead him on, to make him think we could be something we can't.*

But despite her regular mental admonition, Ivy

still found herself jumping when the phone rang, listening to the voices as the messages were left on the machine, and hoping against hope that each call was from Ben.

Ivy pushed her way off of the sofa and tossed the comforter aside. *I'll feel better after a hot bath,* she decided. She padded down the hallway to the bathroom, shedding the cutoffs and T-shirt along the way. Stopping in the bedroom, Ivy wound a terrycloth band around her head, lifting the twists so her hair wouldn't get wet as she lounged in the tub. Satisfied that her hair was protected, she filled the tub with steaming water and added gardenia-scented bath beads. Sitting naked on the edge of the tub, Ivy tested the water with her feet before submerging her body.

As she eased into the tub, she felt some of the tension seep out of her soul. She lay back and allowed the water to cover her up to her shoulders.

The shrill ring of the phone shattered the peace of the moment.

"Go away," Ivy muttered, sinking farther into the tub. She could faintly hear her outgoing message and then the beep. Expecting either Keith's or her mother's voice, she was only partially listening to the message that was being left.

"Hi, Ivy. Sorry I missed you." The voice belonged to Ben. "I hadn't talked to you in a few days, and I wanted to check and see how you were doing."

Ben! The name screamed across her mind. She scrambled to get out of the tub, sloshing water onto the bathroom floor in the process. Soggy footprints marked her path from the tub to her bed. She dove across the bed, trying to reach the phone on the nightstand before Ben hung up.

"Hello? Ben? I'm here!" she all but screamed into the phone.

"Ivy? I thought I had missed you." Ben sounded genuinely pleased.

"I was just . . ." She hesitated, unsure how to explain herself. *If I tell him I was in the tub, he'll know I got out just to talk to him. If I tell him I was screening calls, he'll know he got through the screen.* In that split second, she decided that no explanation was the best course of action.

"It's good to hear from you." She hoped she sounded sincere but casual. "How have you been?"

"I'm doing fine, but the question is, how have you been?" Ben's voice was like a warm caress. "I know you start back to work tomorrow, and I know that won't be very easy for you. I wanted to call to say I'm here for you if you need me."

Warmed by his concern and thoughtfulness, Ivy dropped all pretense of casualness as a sigh escaped from her lips. "That is so very sweet. I don't know what I've done to deserve a friend like you, but I'm so glad you are in my life."

Ben chuckled self-consciously. "I'm just happy I can help you. Hey, I have a thought——why don't I come to your office tomorrow and take you to lunch? By lunchtime, you will probably be ready for a break. How 'bout it?"

Ivy didn't hesitate. "I would love to have lunch with you tomorrow." *I've paid my penance,* she thought defiantly. *Time for the period of mourning to come to an end!*

The conversation ended with them confirming the next day's plans. Ivy hung up and slid off the bed to return to her bath. She smiled at the body-sized wet spot she'd left on the bedspread.

The things we do for love. . . . The thought stopped her cold. *Love? I don't think so!* She dismissed the thought as ridiculous, and climbed back into her now tepid bath. *Love? Right!*

Eleven

In the week that followed, Ben and Ivy fell into a comfortable routine. He would go into downtown Chicago every day and meet Ivy for lunch. Ivy had insisted on what she called a "buffer zone" between her office and their lunches, an area where they were unlikely to run into any of her coworkers or friends.

"I don't want anybody in my business any more than they already are," she'd declared. Her strategy had paid off; they had not run into anyone who might raise an eyebrow at the sight of their innocent lunches.

Ben respected her choice but still felt she was overcompensating. "If people have a problem, it's their problem, not yours," he often repeated. "Maybe so," Ivy countered, "but I have no intention of being the object of any more gossip." Ben had shrugged and made himself available to meet her at the restaurants of her choosing.

Ivy felt her life was almost back to normal. After the initial round of sympathetic words and pitying looks when she'd first returned to the office, her coworkers had not mentioned the canceled wedding or its aftermath again. She was back in contact with her friends, and remarkably, they had all grown closer. Even her mother had settled down and seemingly made her peace with Ivy's life choices. The only fly in the ointment was Keith.

"He is still calling me and coming by the apartment," Ivy confided to Ben during one of their lunches. She toyed with her pasta, pushing the rotini around on her plate with her fork. "It's like he doesn't realize we've broken up."

"How could he not realize it?" Ben looked up from his lasagna, a perplexed expression on his face. "You left him at the altar . . . can you be more clear than that?"

Ivy shook her head. "You wouldn't think there could be any question after that, but Keith is determined to act like I'm just on some kind of relationship sabbatical, and when I get back, I'll be ready to pick up where we left off. And now that the weekend is coming, I'm willing to bet he'll try even harder to get in touch with me. I don't get it. I don't know what else I can say to make myself clear."

Ben made no effort to hide his disgust. "Don't say anything else," he advised. "You just go on about your business and live your life. Either he'll get it or he won't, but you can't let his obstinacy determine how you're going to act."

"That's much easier said than done," Ivy sighed. "I don't want to keep hurting Keith—"

"You are not hurting Keith," Ben interrupted. "Keith is hurting himself. Don't let him pressure you into doing something you don't want to do. If you're still convinced you made the right decision, stick to it—no matter how sad and pathetic Keith acts."

In the back of his mind, Ben knew his advice was at least partially self-serving—the last thing he wanted was for Ivy to weaken under Keith's onslaught. But he honestly believed she would be better off without Keith, and it was time for her to face some hard realities.

"How did I know you were going to say something like that?" Ivy teased.

"Because I keep saying something like that. Because you keep having this same problem." Ben's impatience was beginning to show. "Ivy, you deserve so much better than that jerk. When will you start living the life you want and stop trying to please or placate everybody else?"

Ivy sat back in the booth, stunned by his words. "That's a little harsh, isn't it?"

"I don't think so." Ben was on a roll now. "Somebody needs to tell you the truth. You made a courageous and painful decision, but now it's time to put it behind you and move on." He stopped short of saying "move on with me," although the words burned in his heart. "I mean, look around you. You selected this out-of-the-way restaurant because you want to have lunch with me, but you don't want to be seen with me. And why is that? Because you don't think people will understand. So what? Time to press on, Ivy. The sooner you get back to leading a normal life, the sooner your life will get back to normal."

"I owe it to Keith to be as gentle and discreet

as possible. I embarrassed him enough at the wedding; there's no reason to add insult to injury."

"And when do you get to start doing what you want to do? How long do you have to keep making choices based on what's going to be best for Keith or your mother or your friends?" Ben grabbed the check and rose to leave. He tossed a bill on the table to cover the check and the tip and shoved his wallet back in his pocket. "I'm going to go now, before I say something I regret. Besides, you probably have to get back to work. You don't want to be gone too long—that might give your coworkers something to talk about."

Ivy watched as he stalked out of the restaurant, obviously annoyed. She was still wrapped in the stunned surprise that settled over her at Ben's words.

What happened to gentle Ben? she wondered. *Why is he so upset? I'm just trying to do the right thing. He has always understood that before. . . .*

Checking her watch, she realized that it was in fact time to get back to work. Resolving to call Ben later, she slid out of the booth and left the restaurant.

When Ben arrived at his apartment, he was still seething from his lunch with Ivy. He tried to understand rationally why he was so upset, but eventually he gave up and accepted that "rational" had nothing to do with what he was feeling.

Still Keith . . . after everything that's happened, and all the time we've spent together, she's still worried about

Keith! Frustration welled in Ben's throat. *How did I wind up in this place—serving as friend and confidant? Good ol' safe buddy Ben,* he thought derisively. *She must see me as some kind of sexless eunuch.*

The sound of his doorbell interrupted his self-flagellation. He snatched open the door, startling the postman on the other side.

"Uh, I have a certified letter for Benjamin J. Stephens." The mailman held out a writing board with a thin envelope clipped to it.

"I'm Ben Stephens," Ben said as he scrawled his name in the indicated spaces. Ben accepted the letter and a small stack of other mail from the postman. With a slightly apologetic smile, Ben closed the door and looked down at the correspondence in his hands.

Ben tossed the stack of mail onto his dinette table, ignoring for the moment the usual collection of bills, catalogs, and flyers. His attention instead was riveted to the thin business-sized envelope that bore the return address of the Julian Foundation. He fingered the envelope, turning it front and back, as if he could somehow discern the envelope's contents without actually breaking the seal.

"This is it." His voice filled the empty air around him. "Am I going to Africa or not?" Unexpectedly, Ben realized that he wasn't ready for the answer to that question. He realized suddenly that either result would carry its own measure of bad news. "Africa or Ivy. . . ." Ben placed the envelope on the table facing up. He pulled out one of the chairs, spun it around so that the back was facing him, and straddled it as he settled down in front of the envelope. "Africa or Ivy," he repeated softly. He traced the outline of the envelope absently. It was a false choice, and intellectually he knew that—Ivy had made it abundantly clear that they could only be friends, and this fellowship was something he had worked very hard to achieve. But even though his mind understood the priorities, his heart was working on its own agenda.

During the time he'd spent with Ivy, Ben found his affection for her growing. He admired her self-determination and her drive to remake her life. He could see glimpses of the woman she would become, and he had hopes of being much more than that woman's "buddy" Ben.

But if I'm gone for six weeks, what'll happen to our relationship then? Ben grimaced, thinking of the still-persistent Keith. *Six whole weeks for him to sweat Ivy . . . six weeks without me around.* After a moment, Ben shrugged. *This is stupid. Keith had two whole years without me around and he wasn't able to close the deal. Ivy's gonna do whatever she chooses— whether I'm in Liberia or North Side Chicago.*

With a resigned sigh, Ben slid his finger under the corner of the sealed flap and opened the envelope.

"Dear Mr. Stephens," he read aloud. "The Julian Foundation is please to notify you that you have been accepted into the Teachers for Africa Fellowship program."

A grin that seemed to start at his core and spread until it encased his whole body spread across his face. "Yeah!" he exclaimed. Elation filled him as he pumped his fist in the air triumphantly.

His previous hesitancy forgotten, Ben read the letter further for the details.

"Two weeks?! They want me to leave in two weeks?" His mind raced as he began to catalog all that would have to be done in the next two weeks. He jumped up from his chair and reached for the phone, intending to call his parents to share his good news. As he dialed his parents' number, a certain cocoa-colored face framed by shiny black twists of hair appeared in his mind's eye.

I wonder what her reaction will be? The thought blazed across his mind before he could rein it in. An elegant shrug signaled his feelings. *If it's meant to be,* he decided, *six weeks in Africa won't stop it.*

"Hello?" His mother's voice broke into his thoughts.

"Ma! Have I got news for you. . . ."

Keith was having a very bad week. Like Ivy, he too had to go back to work after his week's "honeymoon." But unlike Ivy's experience, his coworkers at the bank were not nearly as sympathetic. While no one had been bold enough to laugh in his face —he was a vice president, after all—several times during the week he had caught glimpses of people whispering behind their hands, pointing, and chuckling. He had walked into the break room on at least two occasions and people had abruptly stopped their conversations. While it was entirely possible that these incidents had nothing to do with Keith's aborted wedding, he was feeling extremely humiliated and exposed so that possibility never occurred to him. He was convinced that everyone at the bank, from his fellow vice presidents to the tellers in the lobby, was talking about how he was jilted at the altar.

Other attention was directed toward him also. The several women in the office who had always maintained a polite professionalism were suddenly offering to be there for Keith if he needed someone to talk to. One of the women had offered to come to his apartment and fix him a home-cooked meal. And one financial analyst in his department had even offered him a hot oil massage, "to work the stress out of your back."

While Keith did not consider himself a conceited man, he was astute enough to realize when he was being hit on. He found their attentions both distracting and annoying. He resented having to fend off their advances almost as much as he resented being the object of office gossip.

I was supposed to be a newlywed by now, showing off my honeymoon pictures and telling everybody how wonderful marriage is, he fumed. *How can the bank's board of directors see me as an up and comer if I can't even manage to get my bride down the aisle?*

Added to his frustrations at work was the frustration he felt trying to get through to Ivy. She had so far not returned any of his calls, not acknowledged the flowers, not answered the intercom when he showed up at her door.

He checked his watch. *She must be back from lunch by now,* he thought. He reached for the phone but then drew his hand back. *I am not up to leaving another message with her secretary.* He leaned back in his leather desk chair and steepled his fingers under his chin.

It's Friday, and I don't feel like facing any more rejection tonight. After a moment, he reached for the phone and placed a different call.

"Hello?"

"Hi," Keith forced a smile into his voice. "How have you been?"

"Well, how nice of you to ask," the female voice was chilly. "I haven't heard from you since you got back from Hawaii. Why is that?"

"I'm sorry," Keith deflected the question. "It's just been a very hectic time for me. I had hoped you of all people would understand that. You can't imagine what I've been going through these last two weeks."

Immediately contrite, the woman changed her tone. "I'm sorry, Keith. I didn't mean to come down on you. I am glad you called. What can I do for you?" The question was low and suggestive.

Keith smiled and relaxed a bit. "Well, actually, someone here at the bank offered me a hot oil massage. That sounded like a great suggestion, but not from her. I don't suppose you know how to give a massage, do you?"

"Massages are my specialty," she answered. "Come over tonight?"

"I'll be there right after work. See you then." Keith replaced the receiver on its hook.

That ought to help me rejuvenate and gear up for Project Ivy, he thought. *I just need to recharge, and then I'll be ready to help Ivy come to her senses.* He smiled in anticipation of the night ahead.

Twelve

On Saturday morning, Ivy was pleasantly surprised that the voice on the other end of her intercom belonged to Ben. She had tried to reach him the night before, but had been unsuccessful. She was afraid he was still annoyed from their lunch the day before. After pressing the buzzer to open the downstairs security door, Ivy opened the door to her apartment and stood there to greet him.

"Hi, Ben." Ivy smiled warmly. "This is a nice surprise. What brings you by?"

"I have some news," Ben began.

"Good news, I hope?" Ivy cocked her head to the side as she stepped aside to allow him to enter the apartment.

"Well, I think it's good news; we'll just see what you think about it." Ben quickly told her all about the Julian Foundation fellowship.

"You're going to Africa?" Ivy felt numb. "For six weeks? When do you leave?"

"In about two weeks. They're expecting me in Liberia by the end of the month."

"Two weeks? That doesn't leave us much time. I mean, leave *you* much time . . . to get ready, I mean." She stumbled over the hasty clarification. She paused for a moment, trying to get her bearings, raw confusing emotions raging inside her. *Ben's leaving me! What will I do for six weeks without him?*

When she collected her thoughts, she managed a weak smile. "That sounds like a great opportunity for you, Ben. You must be very excited."

"I am. It's something I've always wanted to do."

"Why didn't you mention it before now?" Ivy hoped the question sounded casual. "This is the first I've heard of a teaching fellowship."

Ben shrugged. "I guess I didn't want to jinx it, you know, by talking about it before I'd heard anything."

"Oh, I see." Ivy lowered her eyes to hide the sadness she knew must be mirrored in them. "Well, you're going to have a lot to do in the next two weeks. If there's anything I can do to help, let me know."

"Thanks, Ivy. I really appreciate that. My mom and sisters are helping me pack, but I'll have a lot of other things to attend to before I can leave the country for six weeks. I might take you up on your offer."

Ivy nodded, eyes still downcast. "Well, you just be sure you do. I'm willing to help you however I can."

They stood silently for a few long moments, neither quite sure what to say next. Ben finally cleared his throat, breaking the strained silence.

"Well, I'm going to go now. My mom has sent me to get packing tape and boxes. I'm afraid to

think about what she's planning to send to Liberia
with me. Probably toilet paper and socks, like I'm
going to war or something." He chuckled to
lighten the moment.

"Um, OK." Ivy moved back to the door and
reached for the knob. "I'll talk to you soon." It
wasn't what she wanted to say, wasn't what her
heart was urging her to say, but it was all she could
manage to say.

If Ben was disappointed by her reaction to his
news, he gave no sign. With a gentle smile, he bent
to kiss her cheek. "Talk to you soon," he said, and
then he eased out the door.

Liberia! Ben's going to Liberia for six weeks? Ivy
leaned her head against the door, unable to say
why the news that had been so good for Ben was
so bad for her.

The two weeks before his departure passed in a
blur. Between her job during the day and the errands and packing she helped Ben with in the eve-
nings, Ivy's time was full and busy. Too busy, in
fact, to dwell on her own feelings of impending
loss at the thought of Ben leaving. Far too soon,
it was Ben's last night in Chicago. He was booked
on a seven o'clock flight the following morning.

"Can I cook you a farewell dinner?" She called
him from work early on the day before he was
scheduled to leave.

"I don't know," Ben teased, "can you? I mean
I've never seen you cook, or even heard you talk

about cooking. I'm not sure I want my last American meal to be a TV dinner."

"Very funny, Mr. Stephens. I'll have you know I'm an excellent cook—I just don't do it often, that's all. But for your last night in town, I'll pull out all the stops. So how about it? Dinner tonight?"

Ben hesitated for a split second, thinking about the farewell dinner his mother had planned at her home. Acknowledging that as much as he loved his family, he'd rather spend his last night with Ivy, Ben immediately accepted her offer.

"Dinner sounds great. What time should I come by?"

"Actually, I was thinking I'd get some groceries and come to your place. I thought you might still have some last-minute packing to do, and this way you can finish packing while I cook. Would that be all right?" Ivy unconsciously held her breath, waiting for his response.

"Well, yeah. That sounds like a great suggestion. I have to warn you, though, most of my cooking stuff has been packed away."

"No problem," Ivy breathed easier. "I'll be sure to bring everything I'll need. Eight o'clock?"

"Eight will be fine," Ben assured her. "See you then." He ended the call and immediately phoned his mother. "Ma? Something's come up. Would it be possible for my farewell dinner to be a farewell lunch?"

"Oh, Bennie, I don't know," Judy hesitated. "Your sisters are planning to come here after work. I'm not sure if they can get here much sooner than that. What's going on? Why are you trying to change our plans?"

"It's not that big a deal," Ben stalled. "I've got some last-minute packing to do, and I just wanted to be home early, that's all."

"That's not all, Bennie. Now tell your mother the truth—you've got plans, don't you? With that mystery woman you've been spending so much time with, but won't introduce me to. Am I right?"

Ben laughed. "Ma, there are so many things going on in that statement that I'm not sure where to even begin to respond. First off, I am telling the truth—I want to be home so I can get finished with all my packing. And yes, Ivy and I have plans for tonight. But she's no mystery woman. She's just a good friend."

Judy harrumphed. "She must be some kind of good friend for you to kick your family to the curb to spend your last night in America with her. Why haven't you introduced me to this friend of yours?"

"It just hasn't come up, Ma. I'm not trying to hide her from you or anything. There's not really any reason for you to meet her, actually. She's only a friend."

"What? I don't get to meet your friends?" Judy snorted. "And I don't care what you say, Bennie, this woman is more than a friend to you. But never mind," she changed the subject. "What do you want me to do about dinner? I'm sure Dionne and the kids can't get here before five o'clock."

"Then let's make it five," Ben said. "But I'll have to leave by seven or so, OK?"

"Guess it'll have to be. I've got to go . . . I have

to call your sisters and tell them about the change in plans."

"Thanks for understanding, Ma." Ben hung up the phone, feeling a little guilty about slighting his family, but his guilt was overshadowed by his anticipation of the evening with Ivy. He hurried to his bedroom to try and finish as much of the packing as possible so he would be free to concentrate on Ivy.

Ivy's afternoon at work was shot. She tried to focus on the reports on her desk, but her mind was elsewhere, planning the meal she would prepare that night for Ben. *It has to be special,* she thought, *special but easy because I do not want to spend all night in the kitchen.* She cut off her thoughts before she could examine exactly where she did want to spend the night.

The phone on her desk rang, interrupting her musings. She craned her neck to look at the desk outside her door. The desk was empty; her secretary must have taken a coffee break. The phone rang again, attracting Ivy's attention. Thinking that it might be Ben calling back, she answered the line.

"Ivy Daniels."

"Well, this is a nice surprise. I expected to be screened by your secretary again."

"Hello, Keith." Ivy's tone was flat. "What can I do for you?"

Keith's dry chuckle sounded through the phone. "What can you do for me? That's pretty funny, Ivy.

You could return my calls, answer your door, acknowledge my flowers—in general, you could stop avoiding me."

Ivy rolled her eyes. "I've been avoiding you because I was trying to spare you any more pain, but you just won't leave well enough alone. It's been a month now since we didn't get married. How much longer do you plan to keep this up?" Ivy paused for a moment, gathering steam. "So you know what, Keith? There is something you can do for me. You can back off, get a clue, and accept that our relationship is over."

The phone line hummed as silence stretched between them. Finally, Keith found his voice.

"I have been waiting for you to wake up and realize what you've done. I've been trying to be patient while you sorted out whatever demons were keeping you from realizing that we belong together. But I am not going to keep begging you, and I am not going to keep opening myself up to be dissed by you. So I hear you, Ivy—I've got my clue. You won't be hearing from me again. But when you look around at the mess you've made of your life, and you want to try and fix it, give me a call. I might be willing to help you."

He slammed down the phone, creating an ear-shattering reverberation that made Ivy jump.

Ivy jerked the receiver away from her ear and stared at it. Mixed emotions churned inside her. Guilt that she'd hurt Keith once again and sadness that the relationship was finally over fought for prominence, but the one emotion that surfaced with the most force was pride. She was proud of herself for doing what she needed to do for herself, and damn the impact on others. She was proud that she'd stood her ground and handled the situation, not by avoiding Keith, as she had been trying to do, but by saying what she meant and meaning what she said.

A slow smile spread across her face as she replaced the receiver on its hook. *Time to make some choices that will be to my benefit. Ben was right—the sooner I get back to leading a normal life, the sooner my life will get back to normal.*

She switched off the computer on her desk and reached into the bottom drawer to retrieve her purse. Turning off lights as she went, Ivy closed her office door and stopped at her secretary's desk.

"Allison, good you're back. I'm taking the rest of the day off." The smile broadened slightly. "If there is an emergency, I can't be reached, so someone else will have to handle it. Have a good weekend, and I'll see you Monday."

She practically bounced down the hall to the elevator. *I've got to make plans for dinner tonight.* Humming softly, she began preparing a grocery list in her head.

The farewell dinner at the Stephens' home was hard for Ben. As excited as he was about the fellowship, he knew he would miss his family terribly. Everyone tried to put on a happy face, and even though they all knew it was only for six weeks, an undercurrent of gloom ran through the whole evening. After the meal, which no one ate much of, it was time for Ben to kiss his family good-bye.

"Ben, your mother and I are very proud of you," Greg said as he hugged his son. "Take care of yourself, and be sure to write."

"I promise, Dad." Ben returned the tight hug, grateful that he and his father were not ashamed to embrace each other.

Tracy came next, her eyes bright with unshed tears. "What am I going to do without my big brother for six weeks?" she whined.

Ben hugged her and kissed the top of her head. "You'll be fine. Just stay out of trouble, and I'll be back before you know it."

"Can I get a piece of that?" Dionne approached them. Ben and Tracy opened their arms and pulled her into the circle so that all the Stephens siblings were embracing.

"Don't cry, girls. The time will pass very quickly. You guys take care of Mom and Dad for me, OK?"

"That goes without saying, little brother," Dionne said. "You just worry about taking care of yourself. Watch out for head-hunting cannibals."

Ben threw his head back and laughed. "I'm not Tarzan going into the jungle, Dee. I'm going to a small town in Liberia, where I'll stay in the sponsor's house. But I promise, if I see any headhunters, I'll duck!"

Giggles rang out in response to Ben's words. After hugging his nephews and promising to bring them back something wonderful, Ben turned to say good-bye to his mother.

"I know, it's only six weeks, and you'll be back

before we know it, and you'll take good care of yourself." Judy gave her son a weak smile. I'm going to miss you, Bennie."

"I know, Ma."

Ben and Judy embraced, both fighting back tears. After a moment, Judy pulled away, swiping at her eyes. "I almost forgot, I have something for you." She left the room and came back, struggling under the weight of a heavy cardboard box. Ben hurried over to her to take the box from her hands.

"Ma! Is this what I think it is?"

Just as Ben had expected, his mother had prepared a care package for him, filled with essentials she was convinced he'd need while in Liberia. Ben shook his head and smiled.

"Ma, I don't know what I'd do without you." He bent slightly and kissed her cheek. "Now I really do have to get going."

"Tell me again why you won't let your father and me take you to the airport," Judy insisted.

"It would just be too much hassle for you guys to come all the way into the city to get me, and then drive all the way out to the airport. One of my friends will take me in the morning. It'll be easier that way."

"One of your friends? It wouldn't happen to be this mystery lady you won't introduce me to and who made you change your plans with your family, would it?" Judy placed her hands on her hips as she talked.

"No. Ma. The friend who's taking me in the morning is Darryl. And Ivy's not mysterious. I just haven't seen a need to expose her to all of you yet," he teased. "Now give me a kiss and wish me luck so I can go."

Judy sighed. "You know we'll all be praying for you." She wrapped her arms around his neck and squeezed. "Make sure to write us and let us know how it's going." She kissed both cheeks and released him.

Ben gave them all one last encouraging smile and then left to finish preparing for his excellent adventure.

Turkey tetrazini, Ivy decided. *It's elegant, delicious, and easy to make.* She propped open the cookbook so she could see the list of ingredients she'd need for the dish. After checking her cabinets and refrigerator, she quickly made a grocery list. She paused for a split second, then added white Grenache wine to the list. *What's dinner without wine?*

She then focused her attention on her closet. What to wear to Ben's apartment had weighed on her mind all afternoon. *Nothing too dressy*, she thought as she scanned through the closet. *It needs to be casual and comfortable; I did promise to help him finish packing and cook dinner, so I'll be working. And it has to be cool; it's Chicago in July. But not my usual work-around-the-house clothes; it has to be something I look nice in, too.*

She stood pondering with her arms folded across her chest for several minutes. *Oh, this is silly*, she scolded herself. *Pick something and go!* She finally decided on a pair of khaki belted walking shorts.

She added a ruby-colored silk tank and a pair of flat sandals. Satisfied, she headed to the bathroom to get ready.

Thirteen

At promptly eight o'clock, Ivy juggled two bags and rang Ben's doorbell. A smiling Ben answered so quickly it seemed as though he had been waiting by the door for her arrival. Ivy's breath caught in her throat at the sight of him. He was wearing what she assumed to be his working clothes: a sleeveless black T-shirt and long basketball shorts with the Chicago Bulls logo embroidered on the hem. But it wasn't the clothes that had her momentarily speechless, it was the way Ben wore the clothes. With no sleeves, the distinctive cut of muscle was evident in his biceps. Because of the shorts, even though they came down to his knees, she could see the firm curve of calf muscle in his leg. It was the first time she had ever seen his legs, she realized. The elastic waistband of the shorts emphasized his slim waist. The black color of the clothes was a perfect contrast to his warm, honey-colored skin. He wasn't wearing his glasses, so she had an unobstructed view of his soulful eyes. For the first time, she noticed tiny flecks of gold in the hazel pupils. This casual "Ben at home" was a whole new side that she had never seen before. He appealed to her in a way that she had never felt before when looking at Ben.

"Hi," he said. "Let me take those." He eased the bags out of her arms. "What have you got in here? Cooking for an army tonight?"

Ivy found her voice. "You said I'd need cooking utensils and stuff, so I brought pots and measuring spoons, and whatever else I could think of. My mother always says it's better to have it and not need it than need it and not have it."

"Well, it sure looks like you've got everything but the kitchen sink in here. Fortunately for you, I've got one of those." He gestured with his head. "Come this way and I'll lead you to it."

She closed the apartment door and followed him to the kitchen. Along the way, she made note of the decor, admiring the masculine colors and fabrics he'd chosen for his furniture. Butterscotch-colored leather covered the sofa and matching club chair. An oak entertainment cabinet took up most of one wall and was filled with a variety of electronic equipment. Oak coffee and end tables completed the comfortable room. What impressed Ivy most about the space he'd created were the pictures. He had dozens of frames, some holding family portraits taken at professional sittings, but most filled with candid snapshots. The frames sat on each table, and some hung on the walls.

"This is the first time I've ever been in your apartment," she commented. "It's very nice. Did you take all those pictures?"

"Most of them," he answered. "Photography is a hobby of mine. I guess I inherited that from my mother. She's a real stickler for photos; she insists we take some nearly every time we're together."

"I think that's great. That way you capture your family history. You'll have to show me some of them later."

"I'd love to." He backed into the kitchen door to open it, and held it open for Ivy to enter. He set the bags on a counter.

"This is it," he said. "It's small, but it's serviceable. Do you need anything?"

"I don't think so. I'm pretty sure I've got everything in my bags, but I'll yell if I do need something." She shooed him out. "You have to go now so I can get busy. Dinner'll be ready in about an hour."

"What're we having?"

"Turkey tetrazini. I hope you're hungry."

Thinking about the huge dinner his mother had fixed, most of which went uneaten, Ben could only smile. "I can't wait."

"Good. Now go on, don't you have some packing to do?"

"Actually, yes. I thought I was finished, then my mother gave me this huge box of stuff. Now I've got to figure out how to get it in my bags." He moved toward the door. "So I'm going to leave you to your cooking while I try and get this stuff packed."

"Good idea," Ivy agreed. "Go on," she shooed. "I'll call out if I need you."

Ivy unpacked her bags and laid out all her supplies. After checking over her shoulder to make sure Ben was gone out of the kitchen, she pulled out the recipe page she'd torn from the cookbook and set to work.

Ben stood in his bedroom facing an already over-stuffed footlocker into which he had to make room for the Judy Stephens care package. He tried to focus on the task at hand, but his mind kept wandering—back to his kitchen, to be precise.

Damn, she looks good! The thought kept repeating in his mind. He could feel his pulse quickening as he pictured the khaki shorts, which exposed her beautifully shaped legs; the jewel-toned tank, which perfectly complemented her cocoa-colored skin; and the vibrantly shiny twists of hair that crowned her head. He longed to smooth his hands over her hair to see if the twists felt as soft as they looked. And then there was that tattoo—that sexy as hell tattoo that encircled her arm, embellishing the toned muscle underneath.

Down, boy. Ben took a deep breath and tried to reign in the ache he felt before it raged out of control. *We're just friends, remember. That's the way she wants it, and that's the way it will be. She's just a pal who came to wish me bon voyage.* Ben repeated the words in his head until they were almost like a mantra, but the pep talk was doing little good. His arms still ached to hold her; his lips couldn't help but wonder what it would be like to kiss her; and his groin—well, Ben made a conscious effort not to focus on the desires of his groin, just in case the loose-fitting basketball shorts were not loose enough to conceal his growing need.

With a frustrated groan, Ben forced himself to tackle the packing job, hoping the physical activity would redirect his energies. He opened the box his mother had given him and could only shake his head with amusement at the contents.

The several bottles of water were the source of most of the box's weight. Judy had also included two flashlights, batteries, several rolls of film, a couple of cans of bug spray and stationery with stamped envelopes addressed to Mr. and Mrs. Gregory Stephens.

And people say I'm a boy scout. Mom's the ultimate personification of "always prepared." Ben reached into his footlocker and started rearranging its contents to make room.

In the kitchen, Ivy was finishing up her preparations. The turkey tetrazini was in a casserole dish, ready to go into the oven. She set the oven temperature and slid the dish in. She quickly cleaned up the mess she'd made and put all of her supplies back into the bags. She looked around the kitchen to make sure everything was as she'd found it. Satisfied, she wiped her hands on a dish towel and headed out of the kitchen in search of Ben.

She walked into the living room and called for him. "Ben? Where are you? Is everything all right?"

A muffled grunt was her answer. "Ben?" She headed down the hall in the direction of the grunt. Entering his bedroom, she found him struggling with the closure on a footlocker. She couldn't help but giggle at his predicament.

He looked up at the sound. "I'm glad you're so entertained." He made a face. "But are you gonna help me, or just keep laughing?"

"You know, the problem is you've got too much stuff in that trunk."

"You think?" Ben said sarcastically.

Completely unfazed by his sarcasm, Ivy laughed again and crossed the room to help. "I used to travel a lot for my job, and I learned a few packing tricks that might work here. First open that thing and let's see what you've got in there."

Skeptical but desperate, Ben opened the lid **and** moved aside. Ivy quickly began pulling items from the trunk. In short order, she refolded the clothes into much smaller bundles. She reorganized the items in the trunk so that the limited space was used more efficiently. Ben moved in to help, and she gave him directions about which piece went in which spot. Soon all of Ben's things, including the items from his mother, were in the footlocker. Impressed, he closed the lid. The lip popped open. Frustrated, he tried to force the lid closed again, and again it resisted his efforts.

"It's still too full," he complained. "I can get it closer to being locked than before, but the lid still won't close all the way."

"Hang on," Ivy said. "Let me sit on it, and then you snap the lock in place once the lid is all the way down."

Ben nodded and stepped away so she could sit on the lid of the trunk. Ivy eased over to the trunk and pushed the lid down. It popped back up. She tried again, and found it impossible to hold the lid down and climb on the trunk at the same time.

Ben watched for a few moments, laughter building in his throat at the scene before him. Ivy's good humor, however, faded a little bit every time the lid popped open.

"Tell you what—how 'bout you get some duct tape and strap this thing closed?" Ivy suggested.

"Well, if it didn't have to make it several thousand miles across the world, that might work. But I think we're going to have to figure something else out." Ben knelt in front of the trunk. "Here, I'll hold it down, and you climb on." He placed his hands on the lid and pressed his body weight onto it. Ivy watched for a moment, making sure the lid really was down and wouldn't fly up when she tried to sit on it. Convinced it was safe, she scooted onto the lid of the footlocker. Ben released his hold slowly; Ivy's weight was enough to hold the lid securely in place. He bent to the lock. The lock was in the center front of the trunk, so Ivy had to move her legs to the side so Ben could reach the lock. He reached for a nearby padlock and slid it into place, brushing against Ivy's legs in the process. The unintentional contact sent tiny surges of electricity through them both. Ben raised up to a kneeling position, placing himself at eye level with Ivy.

"OK," he said huskily, "it's locked. Thanks for your help." He started to move away, but Ivy stopped him with a warm hand on his cheek.

"I'm glad I could help," she replied, stroking her hand along his face.

"Ivy, don't," Ben pleaded.

"You don't want me to touch you?" she sounded hurt.

"Oh, no . . . it's not that." he assured her. "I do want you to touch me, more than you can imagine, but you have insisted that you want us to be friends."

"We are friends, aren't we?"

"Yes," his frustration was mounting, "but that's supposed to be all we are. And if you don't stop now, I can't promise I won't take this *friendship* to another level."

"What level is that?"

"Don't play with fire, Ivy. You might get burned." Ben tried to move away while he still felt like he was in control of his choices.

"No." The single word stopped him in his tracks. She placed her other hand on his cheek. "I don't want you to move away from me; not anymore."

Their eyes locked in an intimate exchange. Without either of them being aware of their movements, they suddenly found themselves separated by just the space of a breath. Ben combed his fingers through her hair slowly, gently smoothing over the black twists. He smiled slightly, pleased to discover the twists were just as soft as he'd imagined.

Their eyes stayed fixed in the intimate stare, looking for permission to proceed or a warning to stop. Ivy finally broke the stalemate, sliding her hands to the back of his neck and guiding him gently past the last obstacle.

Breath escaped from her as their lips met for

the first time. Softly and gently they kissed, their lips moving with infinite tenderness as they grew more familiar. Slowly Ben's tongue eased between them, tracing the outline of her lips. She gasped for breath yet again as his tongue slid between her parted lips and caressed her own with sweet warmth. She opened her mouth fully, drawing him in, deepening the kiss. Ben slid his arms around her back, pulling her body closer to his. Still seated on the footlocker, Ivy parted her legs and the kneeling Ben moved between them as if that were where he belonged. Heat rose from them as passion filled the air around them. Their bodies touched from lip to hip, sending buffeting waves of need along their nerve endings.

Ivy slid her hands along his firm torso, stopping at the hem of his T-shirt. Grabbing the fabric, she pushed it up, exposing his taut belly and smooth chest. She released his lips long enough to ease the shirt over his head. Shirt discarded in a pile on the floor, Ivy traced the solid outline of muscle and sinew that lined his back. A soft sigh escaped from Ben as her fingertips caressed him.

He kissed her again, more urgently this time, and she met his urgency with need of her own. He pulled gently at her silk tank blouse, releasing the hem from the waistband of her shorts. He stood as he pulled the blouse off of her and tossed it aside. Ben reached for her hands and pulled her up to meet him. He brushed his knuckles against the tops of her breasts, which were revealed by the flimsy red lace bra she wore. Never lifting his hands from her, he cupped her breasts and rubbed his thumbs over the lace covering her nipples. He was rewarded by her sharp intake of breath, and the immediate pebbling of her nipples against his thumbs. Her head dropped back, and he bent to claim her lips again. He felt her arms wrap around his waist, pulling him closer. As he had suspected earlier, the basketball shorts were no disguise for his throbbing need. Her hips ground against him, pushing Ben closer to the edge of losing control.

He pulled away slightly, searching her eyes for any hesitancy or uncertainty. There was none. What he saw mirrored in her eyes was a longing and need for the intimacy that is born of trust and familiarity.

A low groan rumbled in his throat as he surrendered to the passion that consumed him. He bent slightly and swept Ivy into his arms. He kissed her again, claiming her lips during the short walk to his bed across the room. He laid her on the bed and stood back, marveling at her beauty. The pale comforter on his bed perfectly highlighted her smooth, cocoa-colored skin. Her eyelids were heavy with passion; her lips slightly swollen from insistent kisses. The scrap of red lace did nothing to hide the hard nipples that strained against the fabric.

She made no move to escape from his scrutiny, instead reveling in the sensation of being embraced by his eyes. After a moment she reached for him, tugging at the waistband of his shorts. He stood stone still as she eased the clothing and his briefs off his hips with one fluid movement. The garments fell in a puddle around his feet; he stepped out of them and his shoes at the same time. Ivy

laid back and took full measure of his magnificent
body, admiring the physique that was not heavily
muscled, but carried not an inch of fat, either. Her
attention was riveted to his throbbing erection, un-
deniable evidence that he wanted her as much as
she wanted him.

Ben lowered himself onto the bed and bent to
kiss her. Suddenly his hands were everywhere on
her body, stroking her smooth skin, gently squeez-
ing her firm breasts. He slipped his hands under
her and released the hook on her bra. He eased
it off and tossed it away. Then his mouth left hers
as his lips moved to claim her breasts. He laved
and suckled first one stony nipple and then the
other, until Ivy was squirming with pent-up need
under his ministrations. He moved away, and she
immediately felt bereft. His hands found the waistband of her shorts and slowly, methodically he un-
buckled her belt and unbuttoned her shorts. A
moan she wasn't aware of slipped from Ivy's lips
as he slid her shorts and panties off. They lay on
his bed, naked and needful, silently declaring their
love with eyes and hands and mouths and tongues.

Ben rolled onto his back and reached into a
drawer on his nightstand. He fished around in the
drawer for a moment, then produced a small foil
packet. Ivy had watched his movements closely, and
slid her hand into his to claim the packet. Word-
lessly, she opened the package and removed its
contents. She pushed on Ben's shoulder, guiding
him onto his back. She grasped his erection with
one hand, smiling as she heard his sharp intake of

breath. She stroked him gently, his hips raised in a responding rhythm.

"You're gonna want to put that on before it's too late." His voice was thick with desire.

Smiling, she rolled the condom into place and slid her hands along his body. Ben could wait no longer. He moved over her, fitting his body between her soft opened legs. He looked deeply into her eyes and then bent to claim her lips at the same moment his shaft penetrated her wet, welcoming warmth. Ivy's back arched and her arms wrapped around his back. They began to move together slowly at first, their bodies finding the rhythm that was uniquely theirs. He pinned her between his arms and buried his face in her hair, savoring the sensation of the soft, scented twists against his skin. He whispered endearments which rumbled up from his chest and fluttered past Ivy's ear, words she felt more than heard.

Wrapping her arms under his and pulling him even closer, Ivy planted kisses along his jawline and neck and shoulder. Their bodies began to move with more urgency as passion drove them to the brink of the abyss. Ben struggled to control himself, wanting their connection to last—until the end of time, if possible. But as Ivy moved closer and closer to her release, she urged him on with her hips, seeking more, faster, harder. Ben surrendered the illusion of control and lost himself in her. Together they reached the edge of the precipice, and rocked by an explosion of passion that consumed them both, they plummeted over.

Ben collapsed against her, gulping in great gasps

of air. Ivy held him close, gently kneading the muscles in his back. Eventually, he leaned up on his elbows and looked down at her. There was so much he wanted to say, but somehow words failed him.

"I know," Ivy crooned, stroking his face with her hand. "I know."

Ben lowered his head to claim her lips one more time, and then slowly moved away to lie next to her.

"I'm hungry," he said when his voice returned. "What's for dinner?"

"Dinner! Ohmigosh!" Ivy rolled off the bed and hit the ground running. She burst into the kitchen and snatched the oven door open. Billows of smoke poured out. In dismay, she grabbed pot holders and rescued the casserole dish from the inferno. She set the dish on the top of the stove and fanned it with her hand. A naked Ben entered the kitchen, laughter in his eyes.

"It's ruined," Ivy whined. "I completely lost track of time and now your special farewell dinner is ruined."

Ben took the pot holders from her hands and pulled her into his arms. "That's OK," he assured her. "I'm glad you lost track of time. Don't worry, we can order a pizza." He released her long enough to reach for the cordless phone. After pressing one of the speed dial buttons, he was connected to his favorite pizza place. Still holding Ivy's nakedness against his, he ordered a large with everything. Once the order was confirmed, he pushed the Off button and replaced the phone.

"They say it will be at least forty-five minutes before the pizza gets here."

"Oh? What do you propose we do until then?"

He ground his hips against hers, allowing her to feel his growing erection. "I'll bet we can think of something. . . ."

Much, much later, Ivy and Ben sat in his living room, sharing the pizza. She was dressed in one of his pajama shirts; he was wearing the matching pants.

"I can't believe this has happened between us the night before you leave for six weeks," she said. "That's some timing we've got."

"I can't believe this has happened between us at all," he replied. "I have to ask, Ivy. What happened to just friends?"

"I don't know for sure," she answered slowly. "I guess I suddenly realized that you were already more than a friend to me. I guess . . ." Her voice trailed off as she struggled to explain to him what she had not yet explained to herself.

"I don't know, Ben," she said finally. "Let's not worry about it now. You're leaving for Africa in"—she checked the clock on his VCR—"about six hours. There will be plenty of time to sort it all out when you get back. OK?"

Reluctantly, Ben nodded. "My friend Darryl will be here to pick me up for the airport at five-thirty A.M.—I've got a seven o'clock flight. Will you stay with me until then?"

Ivy tossed her half-eaten slice of pizza back in

the box and slid along the couch to snuggle against him.

"Absolutely," she answered.

Fourteen

This has to be some kind of mistake. . . . The words formed in her mind before she could find her voice. Wide-eyed, Ivy could feel her jaw hanging down, but couldn't seem to master the muscle movements that would clamp it shut.

In the week since Ben had been gone, Ivy had felt a little out of sorts. She dismissed the feeling at first, believing it was purely emotional and she would feel better once she got used to Ben being out of reach. But after a fifth day of feeling blue, Ivy finally decided to go to see her doctor. What she had expected would be a routine visit with the doctor perhaps prescribing iron pills to shore up Ivy's blood had turned into a waking nightmare.

"Ivy? Are you OK? Can I get you anything?" The doctor's words drifted through Ivy's consciousness, not generating any rational response. She was only vaguely aware of her surroundings—the sterile, peach-colored room, the cool vinyl of the examination table she sat on, the scratchy cloth of the patient gown she'd been provided.

"Ivy?" A face appeared in her field of vision. "I know this must come as a surprise—"

"Surprise?" Ivy's brain finally clicked into gear.

"Dr. Jenkins, surprise is not how I would describe it. Are you sure about this? Couldn't there have been some kind of mistake?" Ivy's voice grew hopeful.

Dr. Jenkins shook her head slowly. "I'm really sorry, Ivy. The results are irrefutable. I know this has come at a bad time for you, but—"

Ivy's harsh laugh cut off the rest of the doctor's words. "Dr. Jenkins, you have *no* idea." Ivy buried her face in her hands. "Pregnant . . ." She finally allowed herself to say the word. She sat for a few moments with her shoulders slumped and her hands still covering her face. As she began to organize her thoughts, she raised her head and faced the doctor.

"How far along?"

Dr. Jenkins checked the chart in her hand. "Well, based on the date of your last period you've listed here, I'd say about six weeks."

"Six weeks," Ivy repeated. "Well, that makes one thing clear, at least," she muttered.

"I'm sorry, I didn't hear you. What did you say?"

"Never mind, Dr. Jenkins." Ivy sighed. "What do I do now?"

"Well," Dr. Jenkins began, "you have several options here of which I'm sure you're well aware—keeping the baby, putting it up for adoption, or terminating the pregnancy. However, if you decide to see this pregnancy to term, we need to begin prenatal care immediately." She opened a drawer and pulled out a bottle of pills. "These are prenatal vitamins. You need to take one each day." She offered the bottle to Ivy.

Ivy sat on the edge of the examination table, her hands folded tightly in her lap, staring at the bottle as if she expected it to spring to life and attack her.

"Just take the vitamins, Ivy." Dr. Jenkins's tone was reassuring. "Accepting them doesn't commit you to anything. It's just important that you have the proper care."

Proper for what? Or for whom? The words burned in Ivy's mind. She sat for a moment longer, then held out her hand and accepted the bottle. Dr. Jenkins immediately turned her attention to Ivy's chart.

"I'll want to see you back here in two weeks for a checkup."

Ivy's eyes narrowed. "You act as if my decision is already made."

"Not at all." Dr. Jenkins shook her head. "But whatever you decide, I'll still need to see you— either for a prenatal visit or to handle the, um, procedure."

"The procedure . . ." Ivy's face fell to her hand again. "I can't think . . . I need time."

"You have some time before you have to decide," Dr. Jenkins said. "But not a lot of time." She placed her hand on Ivy's shoulder. "If you have any questions or just want to talk, I'm here for you."

Ivy nodded. "Thank you." She slid off the table and reached for her clothes, which were draped across a nearby chair. "I have to go now, Dr. Jenkins. I need some fresh air."

"I'm not quite finished yet—"

"It'll just have to wait until next time," Ivy said firmly. "I have to go—now."

Dr. Jenkins nodded her understanding and crossed to the door. "I'll let you leave on one condition. You have to stop at the receptionist's desk and make an appointment for next week." Dr. Jenkins studied Ivy closely, looking for agreement.

Ivy nodded. "I will, I promise."

Dr. Jenkins pulled the door open and turned to leave. She paused and turned back to Ivy. "It's going to be all right. Everything happens for a reason."

Ivy managed a weak smile, remembering Ben and cheesecake for breakfast. "A good friend of mine told me that once. I can only hope both of you are right."

Ivy stumbled out of the doctor's office, her bag loaded with pamphlets and "So You're Pregnant" brochures, the vitamins rattling in the bottle with each step she took. She had made the appointment but refused to say, even to herself, whether the appointment was for a checkup or some other reason.

Once she reached her car, Ivy flung the bag to the backseat, climbed in and folded her arms across the top of the steering wheel. She stared vacantly out the windshield, her mind processing not the view before her, but instead the bombshell Dr. Jenkins had just dropped.

How can this be? Why did this have to happen now? She lowered her head, resting her forehead on her arms. *I'm trying to separate myself from Keith—now with a baby, we'll be connected forever. And what about Ben?* Her heart ached as she thought about Ben and his reaction to this news. *He's a smart guy . . . he'll realize right away that it can't possibly be his baby, his sense of honor will make him back away, and then I'll never see him again.*

She sat silently in that position for several minutes, tears she didn't even feel escaping from the corners of her eyes.

There are several options . . . Dr. Jenkins's voice filled Ivy's mind. Slowly she lifted her head. *I have some decisions to make.* She wiped her face dry and reached for her cell phone, then called one of the numbers stored in its memory.

"C'mon, Kim, pick up," she whispered, half impatiently, half prayerfully. After four rings, an answering machine clicked on.

"Kim, I really need to talk to you. Call me later." Disappointed, Ivy ended the call. She thought for a moment, then made another call. This time her call was answered.

"Cherise? Thank goodness you're home."

"Ivy? Is that you?" Cherise sounded surprised.

"Yeah, it's me. Listen, I need to talk to you, it's kinda important. Can I come by?"

"Now?"

"If that's OK." Ivy tried not to let the desperation she felt reflect in her voice. "I really need some advice."

"Sure, honey. Come on by," Cherise said. "I'll put on some coffee and we'll talk."

"Thanks, Cherise. I'll be there in about ten minutes." Ivy ended the call and quickly started the car.

A short time later, she parked in front of Cherise's apartment building and rang the bell. Cherise snatched the door open.

"Ivy, what's going on?" She came out on the stoop to wrap Ivy in a hug. "You sounded so upset on the phone."

"I got some news today . . . and I'm not sure what to do about it." Ivy's voice was muffled because she had buried her face in the taller woman's shoulder. "I really need to get an objective opinion."

"Then I'm your girl." Cherise pulled back and held the door for Ivy to enter. "Come on in, coffee's hot."

Ivy grimaced as she entered the apartment. "Don't think I'll be drinking any coffee today," she muttered. She headed for the sofa and plopped down. Cherise followed and sat in a chair across from her.

"What's going on, Ivy? You look terrible."

Ivy took a deep breath, trying to decide how to begin. "I guess the best thing to do is just spit it out." She ran her hand over her hair, unconsciously smoothing the shiny twists. "I went to the doctor today. Turns out I'm pregnant." She paused for a moment, and the words hung in the air. "Pregnant," she repeated quietly. "That's the first time I've said it aloud."

Cherise sat back in the chair and choked back a gasp. "Are you sure?"

Ivy nodded slowly. "No doubt about it. Approximately six weeks along, according to the doctor."

"Oh, God," Cherise breathed. She said nothing for several long moments; she simply stared at Ivy with a pained expression on her face. "Don't get mad at me," she said finally, "but whose baby is it?"

"Whose baby?" The words exploded from Ivy's lips. "What the hell kind of question is that?"

"Don't get mad, Ivy," Cherise repeated. "I'm not passing judgment or anything, but I know you and that other guy—Ben, right?—had been spending a lot of time together lately. I just wondered . . ."

"I'm six weeks pregnant, Cherise. Six weeks ago I was busily planning a wedding and supposedly happily engaged to Keith." Ivy shook her head, the anger drained out of her. "There's no question about it—this is Keith's baby."

"But could it have been Ben's baby?" Cherise persisted.

Ivy's brows drew together in confusion. "I didn't even know Ben six weeks ago. How could the baby be Ben's?"

"Well, sometimes the doctors are wrong about how far along. Maybe you're not six weeks pregnant." Cherise leaned forward. "I guess what I'm asking is, is there any possibility that Ben could be the father?"

Ivy paused, trying to fully understand the question. "Are you asking me if I've been intimate with Ben?"

Cherise shrugged. "If you had, that might affect the dynamics of this situation."

A dry, humorless laugh escaped from Ivy. "Affect the dynamics . . ." Her eyes glazed over for a moment as her thoughts traveled back in time.

"Ivy?" Cherise prompted.

Ivy focused on her friend as if suddenly realizing she was still there. "The answer to your question is yes, Cherise. Ben and I did have one night together—one amazing night together—before he left the country. But that was only a week ago. So you see, this baby can't possibly be his." A sorrowful expression colored her features. "So, how does that affect the dynamics?"

"Sounds like you and this Ben had gotten pretty close," Cherise observed.

"Yes," Ivy answered slowly, "we had. I had hoped there might be something between us once he got back from Liberia, but this pregnancy changes all that."

Cherise sat deep in thought for a moment. "It doesn't have to," she said finally. "You have options, you know."

"You're talking about an abortion."

"Well, yeah. I mean consider all the factors at work here: you and Keith are not together anymore, and you'd like to keep it that way. You want to get with Ben, but a baby that's not his will end your relationship before it even starts." Cherise warmed to her topic. "Ivy, whatever else you think about Keith, and however you're feeling about him these days, you know he's not the kind of guy to turn his back on a situation like this. If you have Keith's baby, he'll be a part of your life for the rest of your life. He'll want to be a part of his child's life. Your ties with him will never be severed."

"I had thought about that . . . ," Ivy conceded.

"And consider Ben. He's probably hoping something will come of your relationship, too. How's he going to react when he gets back from Africa and finds you pregnant with another man's child?" Cherise shook her head. "Abortion seems like an obvious solution to me, Ivy. I mean, what else can you do?"

"What else indeed?" Ivy stood abruptly, suddenly feeling a need to be alone with her thoughts. "Thanks for the advice, Cherise, but I've got to go."

"Go?" Cherise scrambled to her feet. "Go where? What are you going to do?"

"I honestly don't know yet," Ivy replied. She reached for her friend's hand and gave it a squeeze. "Thank you for being here for me, Cherise. You've given me a lot to think about."

"Are you going to tell Keith?"

"I suppose I should," Ivy began.

"No!" Cherise's objection was quick and definitive. "I mean, I don't think you should tell him anything until you've figured out what you want to do. Because you know if you tell him, he's going to want you to keep the baby . . . and get back together with him." Cherise shook her head. "You don't need that kind of pressure until you've made up your own mind."

Ivy nodded. "You're probably right." She heaved a heavy sigh. "Seems like I've got a lot to think about." She started toward the door. "Thanks again for being such a good friend, Cherise." Ivy smiled weakly and headed out to her car.

"Think about what I've said," Cherise called from the stoop outside the apartment.

"I will, I promise," Ivy answered. She climbed into her car, started the engine and pulled away from the curb. *What now?* she thought. *What on earth do I do now?*

Fifteen

"Ivy! Pick up the phone! It's Kim! I got your message and I'm returning your call. Pick up!"

When Ivy entered her apartment, she heard her friend's voice on the answering machine, so she dropped her bag and raced to grab the phone.

"Kim? Are you still there?"

"Ivy, thank goodness I caught you. What's going on? I got your message and you sounded very upset."

"Something's happened," Ivy began, "and I need your advice."

"OK. I'll be right there."

Ivy shook her head. "That's not necessary, Kim. I don't want you to come all the way over here; I can tell you on the phone."

"I know you can," Kim insisted, "but I can tell from the sound of your voice this is big, so I want to be there with you. I'm on my way." She hung up the phone before Ivy could lodge any more objections. Ivy smiled, warmed by her friend's concern.

Less than twenty minutes later, Kim was at the door. Ivy pressed the entry button and met her at the top of the stairs.

"You really didn't have to come over here," Ivy began.

"Yes, I did. Sorry, girlfriend, but you look like hell." Kim wrapped her friend in a bear hug. "Now tell me what's going on. Has something happened with Keith?"

"Something like that," Ivy led the way into the apartment. "Have a seat, and I'll bring you up to date."

Kim sat in stunned silence as Ivy shared her news.

"So that's where I am now," Ivy finished. "I'm not sure what I'm going to do. Cherise thinks an abortion is the only solution, but I don't know how I feel about that."

Kim gave a low whistle. "Man, Ivy. When you have a problem, you don't mess around." She shook her head. "I take it you haven't told Keith yet?"

Ivy shook her head. "I wanted to have some idea of what my plans are before I go to him."

Kim nodded. "Well, you asked me, so here's my advice. Ivy, you cannot get an abortion." Ivy's eyes widened in surprise. "I know that's not what you expected me to say, but believe me when I tell you having an abortion affects the rest of your life almost as much as having a baby—except with an abortion, you don't get any of the joy of parenthood." Kim's eyes welled up. "You are too much of a nurturing person to even consider an abortion, Ivy. It would eat you alive for the rest of your days."

"I don't know what to say," Ivy began. "Kim,

you sound like you speak from experience. Is there something you want to talk about?"

Kim shook her head. "It was a long time ago. It was a decision I made without considering all the ramifications. I thought it was the best thing, but I still question the wisdom of that choice." Kim reached for Ivy's hands. "I love you, and I will help you with whatever you decide to do. I just want you to weigh all your options carefully. Having Keith's baby does not necessarily mean having Keith. Millions of women raise babies by themselves, many of them with much less support and fewer resources than you'll have."

Ivy felt the first tears of this ordeal pool in her eyes. "What about Ben?" she whispered. "I'll lose Ben if I have this baby."

"Then Ben was not the one for you." Kim was unyielding. "Ivy, if you end this pregnancy just so you can be with Ben, I believe in my soul that you will eventually come to resent him. And that resentment will eventually end the relationship anyway."

Ivy wiped away the tears that threatened to spill down her cheeks. "I don't know what to do."

"That's OK," Kim assured her. "You don't have to know right now. Don't try to make any decisions until you've thought it all through. And Ivy, I know you said you wanted to think it all through before you told Keith, but I believe he has a right to know what's going on. He may want to have some input into the decision. It's his baby, too."

Ivy nodded slowly. "Kim, you know what his input is going to be. He'll want me to have the baby."

"Probably," Kim conceded. "But whatever, it's his right to be involved. You owe him at least that much."

Ivy sat quietly, processing all Kim had said to her. Kim stood to leave. "I'm going to go and let you sort all this out. If you need me, you know I'm just a phone call away."

Ivy managed a quavery smile at her friend. "Thank you for coming by . . . and thank you for being so open with me."

Kim nodded and let herself out. Ivy barely heard the door close, so deep in thought was she. *Well, now what?* She had hoped that Kim would encourage her to end the pregnancy, but after Kim's talk, Ivy had an entirely new perspective to consider. After a few more minutes of conflicting emotions and turbulent thoughts, Ivy decided she was not ready to decide. She headed to the bathroom to do what she always liked to do when problems arose—take a long, luxurious bath. *Things always manage to seem clearer after a soak in the tub,* she thought.

Two days after she learned of her pregnancy, Ivy was no closer to making a decision about her future. She had managed to maintain the appearance of normalcy, going to her job and handling the mundane details of her life. But the pregnancy was always there, looming in the background like a giant storm cloud.

On this day after work, Ivy was supposed to go

to her parents' house to help her mother with her new computer. Grace had decided that she and Albert needed to join the cyber generation, so even though neither of them had ever even touched a computer before, Grace bought a state-of-the-art system. So far their new toy had sat in the boxes in which it had been delivered because neither of the elder Daniels wanted to attempt to set up the machine. Ivy had promised to come and get the computer up and running, including installing whatever software Grace had purchased and setting up their Internet account.

Ivy was nervous about going because her mother always seemed to have a sixth sense about Ivy's troubles. Ivy seriously doubted her on ability to hide her dilemma from her mother, but she wasn't really ready to discuss the situation with her. Ivy considered calling and rescheduling, but she was sure Grace would see through that and demand to know what was wrong.

My only hope, she decided, *is to do this as quickly as possible and then get out before she suspects anything. Hopefully setting up the computer will be involved enough to keep me busy and distracted.*

After work, Ivy drove to her parents' condominium in Chicago's upscale North Side. Ivy smiled, remembering her parents' decision to move into a condo. Albert had insisted that the last thing he wanted to do in his retirement was cut grass. The only way Grace would agree to give up her comfortable house was if she could have the condo she wanted. So after much searching, Grace had finally found an opening in a fairly expensive, exclusive building. She had been sure Albert would refuse, and she'd get to keep her house. But after one look at the condo, Albert eagerly agreed with her selection. They sold the house and moved two months later. It had been a good decision for Albert and Grace; both of them loved their new home, and Grace often commented that the condo was what she had wanted all along.

As she circled the building for the second time, Ivy grumbled about the one major down side to her parents' condo—too few parking spaces. "Wonder what Mom would say if I just called her and told her I can't find a parking space so we'll have to do this another time?" Ivy's voice filled her car. "I mean, that's a legitimate excuse . . . no parking."

Just as the words left her mouth, a Ford Bronco pulled away from the curb about a half a block away.

Oh, sure, Ivy complained to the fates, *wouldn't let me off that easily, would you?* Resigned to facing her parents, Ivy backed into the parking space and turned off her car. "I'm going to do this quickly, so I can leave quickly," she muttered as she walked toward the building. "No problem . . . no problem at all."

Fortified by her internal pep talk, Ivy entered the building, and using the intercom system in the lobby, called her parents' condo.

"Hi, Dad, it's me."

"Ivy! We've been expecting you. Come on up."

At the sound of the buzz, Ivy pulled open the heavy security door. She entered the elevator and shortly found herself standing in front of her parents' condo. *You can do this,* she told herself. *Just focus on the task at hand and go. Focus and go. . . .*

She had lifted her hand and was about to knock when the door was opened.

"Hi, honey, that was quick." Albert beamed at his daughter. "I was going to meet you at the elevator, but here you are already."

"Hi, Daddy." She hugged him. "You didn't have to meet me; I know the way."

"Of course I didn't have to; I wanted to. It's been so long since we've seen you."

"It hasn't been that long," she said defensively.

"Well, it's been long enough." Albert stepped aside for her to enter. "Come on in. Your mother is very excited about getting her computer up and running."

Ivy smiled at his choice of words. *"Her* computer? You don't plan to use it?"

"I really don't think so," Albert shook his head. "I'm an old dog, and I'm not really interested in learning a new trick."

"Don't pay any attention to him, Ivy." Grace came into the foyer to greet her daughter. "He only thinks he doesn't want to learn anything new. As soon as we get hooked up to that Internet thingy and he can start finding information about anything anytime, we'll have to fight to get him off the computer."

Ivy hugged her mother. "You're probably right, Mom. But the first thing we've got to do is get you to stop calling it *that Internet thingy*—that's very nontechnical of you." She smiled at her parents.

"Now, show me where you want to set up your computer."

Grace shook her head. "What's the rush? I thought we'd have dinner first, and then you could set it up."

"Well actually, Mom, I kinda wanted to get finished so I could head home before it gets too late."

"Too late? Too late for what?" Albert questioned. "Come on, Ivy, stay for dinner. We never get to spend any time with you anymore."

"Yes, Ivy, do stay. We have a lot of catching up to do," Grace added.

"Catching up?" Ivy struggled to appear casual. "Catching up about what?"

"Nothing in particular," Grace said slowly. "We haven't talked much since . . . well, you know since when. I just wanted to have dinner with my daughter. Is that a problem?" She eyed Ivy suspiciously.

With the watchful eyes of her parents on her, Ivy had no choice but to agree. "Dinner will be fine," she said.

The meal turned out to be much easier than Ivy expected. The conversation was light, and even though she didn't eat much, Ivy felt the dinner was a success. Once dinner was over, Grace and Albert began clearing the table.

"Let me help," Ivy offered.

"That's OK, baby," Grace answered. "I'd much rather you go in the spare bedroom and start setting up our computer. I really want to ride the Web tonight."

Ivy chuckled slightly. "That's *surf*, Mom, *surf* the Web. We really do have to work on your vocabulary."

"Ride, surf—whatever. Just get my machine up and running."

"Yes, ma'am." Ivy left the dining room, still smiling. In the spare bedroom, she found a new computer desk and hutch, assembled and waiting for the equipment. The computer system itself was in various boxes around the room. Ivy grabbed a pair of scissors from the supplies neatly stacked on a corner of the desk. *I guess the first thing to do is get these boxes open,* she thought. Using the scissors like a knife, Ivy began to slice through the packing tape on the boxes.

She had been working for about a half an hour when Grace came into the room to check on her. Grace leaned against the doorway, her arms folded across her body. She watched silently for a few moments. Ivy had crawled under the desk and was running the various cables to their proper locations.

"There!" Ivy climbed out from under the desk and wiped her hands on her pants. "It ought to be just about ready," she murmured.

"Do you want to talk about it?" Grace's voice caused Ivy to whirl around.

"Mom! I didn't know you were here. How long you been standing there?"

"Not very long." Grace shook her head. "I wanted to check on you."

"The computer is almost ready. I just need to do a couple of final things—"

"Not the computer," Grace said firmly. "I came to check on *you*. What's going on with you, Ivy?"

Ivy hesitated and looked away from her mother's probing eyes. "What makes you think there's anything going on?"

"Please, I know my child. You have been edgy and distracted ever since you arrived, not to mention you picked over your dinner. Something's obviously bothering you."

"It's nothing, Mom," Ivy began.

"Don't tell me it's nothing," Grace snapped. "Tell me it's none of my business, or tell me you don't want to talk about it, but don't tell me it's nothing. That insults my intelligence and my intuition."

Ivy forced herself to meet her mother's eyes. "OK, Mom. I don't want to talk about it. I will tell you soon, but I'm not ready yet. Is that good enough?"

"Yes," Grace nodded. "I can't act like I'm happy you won't talk to me about whatever's bothering you, but I will respect your privacy. Whenever you're ready to talk about it, I'm ready to listen."

"Thanks Mom. I promise, I'll tell you soon." Ivy crossed the room to hug her mother. "Now, do you want me to show you how to use this computer?"

Grace nodded, and the lesson began.

When Ivy finally reached her home that night, she was exhausted. The stress of her situation, added to the evening with her parents, added to the physical symptoms of early pregnancy all combined to leave her feeling drained both emotionally and physically. Once she entered her apartment, Ivy tossed her briefcase, purse, and the day's mail she'd gotten on her way up the stairs onto the coffee table and headed directly to her bathroom, where she intended to soak in a hot tub indefinitely. She noticed the flashing light on her answering machine, but decided to ignore it for the moment.

In short order, Ivy was up to her chin in scented, steaming bathwater, feeling the tension seep out of her body. She had resolved that she would not think about her troubles while in the tub. The problems would all still be there when the water was gone, she thought. *Whatever I need to deal with will just have to wait—the tub is my retreat.*

Eventually Ivy felt relaxed and rejuvenated enough to emerge from her watery hiding place. Wrapping herself in a thick chenille robe, Ivy went to the kitchen to fix a cup of cappuccino. Cup in hand, she was finally ready to face the outside world. She retrieved the mail from the coffee table and pressed the Play button on her answering machine. She was sorting through the mail when the voice of her friend Cherise filled the room.

"Hi, Ivy. I've been thinking about you a lot lately. I wanted to see if you decided to follow my advice. Really, Ivy, an abortion is your only realistic option. I know it seems harsh, but I'm just thinking of you. OK, call me later." The machine beeped, indicating the end of the message.

I hear you, Cherise, Ivy thought.

The machine continued its playback. Two hang-ups and a call from her office later, Kim's voice rang throughout the apartment.

"Ivy, this is Kim. I called to see how you were doing—and to see if you'd made a decision yet. I just want you to know I'm here for you, whatever you decide. Call me later if you want to talk."

The machine beeped twice; there were no more messages.

Ivy sat down heavily on the edge of her bed. *I'm going to have to decide something soon,* she thought. *If I don't, the decision will be made for me—an abortion can't wait forever.*

"Abortion." She said the word aloud, testing the feel of it. "I can have an abortion and put this whole nightmare behind me." Even before she'd finished the sentence, she knew she couldn't do it. Everything about that option caused her pain—in her heart, in her mind, and in her soul.

"This is my baby!" she declared suddenly, more sure of herself than she'd been since she'd learned the news. "She deserves a chance."

She placed her hand on her still flat stomach. "She . . . I wonder . . ." Ivy smiled then, a full, broad smile that conveyed her sense of rightness and her confidence in her decision. For the moment, she pushed aside concerns about Keith or Ben or her parents or her friends. For the moment, she allowed herself to feel pregnant, to imagine the child growing inside her, the child she would nurture and love and protect from that moment on.

"For the rest of my life," she said softly, rubbing her stomach. "It's you and me for the rest of my life." Tears formed in the corners of her eyes, spilled over her lashes, and rolled gently down her cheeks.

She lifted her hand to wipe her eyes and suddenly remembered the mail clutched in her fist. After drying her tears, Ivy began to sort through the mail. Buried amid the usual collection of bills and direct mail solicitations, she saw a letter in an airmail envelope with unfamiliar stamps and a Liberian postmark.

Ben! The name exploded in her mind. She tossed all the other mail aside and tore into the letter from Ben. She curled up in her comforter and read his account of his job and living accommodations and students. She could practically hear his voice as he described the wonders of his small village outside of the Liberian capital, Monrovia.

Then the tone of his letter changed, and his words left Ivy shaken.

> *Ivy, the night we spent together meant more to me than you can imagine, more than I can properly express. Ever since the first day you stumbled into my life, I have wanted to be more than your friend. I don't know what will happen when I return, but I want you to know that I hope we will find a way to be together.*
>
> *You are constantly in my thoughts—Ben.*

Ivy took a deep breath and reread the closing of Ben's letter. *You are constantly in my thoughts.* . . . Tears threatened again, but this time there was no joy behind them.

"I'm so sorry, Ben," she whispered. "I have to do this. Will you still be my friend when you find out?"

Ivy cried again, this time with an acute sense of loss of what could have been.

Sixteen

I can't put this off any longer. Ivy leaned forward in her office chair. *It's time.*

It had taken Ivy a solid week of introspection, crying, and planning to become comfortable with her decision to have the baby. And her decision to surrender a future with Ben. Now that she felt confident and prepared for whatever the future would hold, she knew she had some people to notify. She reached for the phone on the corner of her desk. Keeping her mind deliberately blank, she punched the long unused numbers that would connect her to Keith's private line.

"Jamison here."

"Uh, hi Keith." Ivy's voice cracked slightly.

"Ivy? Is that you?"

She cleared her throat and tried again. "Yes, it's me."

"Well, this is a switch. What can *I* do for you?" His tone was tinged with sarcasm.

"There's something I need to talk to you about—"

"So talk. I'm listening."

"I would rather have this conversation in person."

"Must be important." Keith sounded hesitant.

"I think it is." Ivy took a deep breath. "Can you meet me after work?"

"I knew this day would come," Keith said smugly. "I knew it was just a matter of time."

"What day would come?" Ivy was confused.

"Nothing—never mind. I don't want to steal your thunder."

"Keith, I don't know what you're talking about, but I guarantee you you're wrong. Can we meet somewhere after work?"

"Sure, Ivy. We'll play it your way. How about Navy Pier?"

Ivy thought about the trendy tourist spot he'd suggested for a moment. *I didn't really want to have this conversation in public, but it's a nice enough day for us to be outside.*

"Ivy? Are you still there?" Keith's voice broke into her musings. "Is Navy Pier OK?"

"Yes, Keith. That will be fine. Six o'clock at the Ferris wheel?"

"See you then."

Ivy hung up and hung her head for a moment. *How am I going to tell you, Keith? And what will you say when I do?*

At six o'clock, Ivy stood near the entrance to the giant Ferris wheel, the most recognizable feature of Chicago's Navy Pier, shifting nervously from one foot to the other. As was typical for a summer night, Navy Pier was teeming with people, both tourists and locals, either eating at one of the many restaurants or shopping at the numerous stores or enjoying one of the many games and activities. But all of that action was lost on Ivy as she rehearsed her speech in her head yet again.

A few minutes after six, long enough to be considered fashionably late, Keith strolled toward her, hands in his pockets.

He looks pretty sure of himself, she thought, slightly irritated. *But he does look good . . . it ought to be a beautiful baby.* She silently admired him; even in shirtsleeves and a loosened tie, Keith cut an impressive figure.

He approached her slowly, making no effort to disguise his appraising stare.

"Hi, Ivy," he said. "You're looking well."

"Thank you. So are you."

The banal conversation somehow managed both to annoy her and soothe her frayed nerves at the same time. "Thank you for agreeing to meet me. It's very important that we talk."

"Sure, Ivy. It's no problem. Are you hungry? Can I buy you dinner?" He gestured in the direction of a nearby restaurant.

"No, Keith. I'm not hungry, and I don't want dinner. Walk with me?"

Keith shrugged. "This is your show," he said. "Lead the way."

Ivy and Keith started to walk along the waterside, moving further away from the crowds. They had walked for several minutes in silence. Ivy was not sure how to begin, and Keith was biding his time. Finally when she judged they were far enough away from other people to have a relatively private conversation, Ivy stopped walking and turned to face him.

"Keith, there's no easy way to say this," she began, "and I'm not sure how you're going to react."

Keith held up a hand, interrupting her. "Ever since you called, I had planned to play hard to get, or make you beg the way you've made me beg." Keith's smile was oily. "But then I decided that would be no way to treat the woman I love. So I'm going to let you off the hook, Ivy. I forgive you and yes, I think we can try again."

Ivy looked at him as if he had suddenly sprouted another head on his shoulders. Once the power of speech returned to her, it was all she could do not to laugh hysterically.

"You are so wrong. That's not what I wanted to see you about," she managed.

Immediately Keith's demeanor changed. He went from open and relaxed to guarded and tense in the blink of an eye. "Well, what did you want?" he demanded.

Ivy took a deep breath and collected her courage. "I have some news," she began. "There's no way to say this except to say it, so here goes: I'm pregnant. I decided it was time for you to know."

Keith took an unconscious step back. "Pregnant?" His eyes widened. "How can that be?"

Ivy succumbed to the nervous giggle that had threatened ever since he'd arrived. "Oh, I think you know how. . . ."

Keith shook his head. "That's not what I meant." He eyed her with suspicion. "Why are you telling me this? What does this have to do with me?"

The levity she was feeling evaporated as quickly as a drop of water on a hot griddle. "What does it have to do with you?" she repeated incredulously. "It has everything to do with you. Because although I am a talented woman, I cannot make a baby all by myself." Her eyes were stern.

"Obviously," he said impatiently. "But how do I know it's mine? What about that other guy?" Keith pretended to search his memory for the name, even though he knew it immediately. "Ben something? How do you know he's not the father?"

"I will not dignify that with a response. And you and I have nothing more to say to one another. I felt like you deserved to know, and now I've told you. Good-bye, Keith." She spun on her heels and began resolutely marching in the other direction.

"Ivy! Wait!" Keith called after her. When she didn't stop, he took off at run to catch her.

"Hang on a minute." He reached for her arm, stopping her retreat. "You can't just drop a bomb like that and then walk away."

"What do you care?" She wrenched her arm out of his grasp and stood with her hands on her hips. "You're not even sure the baby's yours. How could my *bomb* possibly matter to you?"

"I'm sorry, Ivy. That was an amazingly stupid thing for me to say." Keith seemed genuinely contrite. "Its just that that was the last thing I expected to hear from you, and I was caught off guard. I know you're not the type of woman who would do something like that."

Ivy glared at him, not willing to forgive his re-action just yet. "You know, Keith, whatever else happened between us, I was always faithful to you."

"I know," Keith hung his head. "I know, and I am sorry." He looked her in the eyes. "How far along?"

Ivy sighed and relaxed slightly. "About eight weeks. The doctor tells me to expect a little bundle of joy around the beginning of March."

"Eight weeks?! And you're just now telling me?"

"I haven't known for eight weeks," Ivy said de-fensively. "I've only known for about two. And I needed to figure out what I wanted to do before I came to you."

"And what have you decided to do?" Keith seemed to hold his breath, waiting for her answer.

"I'm going to have the baby, Keith." Ivy's tone was firm. "I don't expect you to be involved if you don't want to, but I—"

"Not be involved? Ivy, what are you saying? Of course I want to be involved. That's my baby you're carrying." Keith moved toward her and reached tentatively for her midsection. "May I?"

Ivy smiled slightly and nodded. Keith gently put his hand against her belly. "My baby . . . ," he said in wonder.

"My baby," Ivy corrected.

He chuckled and shrugged. "Our baby."

Telling Keith was a walk in the park compared to how telling her parents might turn out, Ivy thought. She stood outside their condo building fidgeting nervously as she waited to be buzzed in. After she left Keith, she went immediately to her parents' home. She knew Keith would be shouting the news from the rooftops, but Ivy wanted her parents to hear it from her first.

After an elevator ride that seemed to last an eternity, Ivy knocked on her parents' door. A smiling Albert admitted her.

"Well, isn't this a pleasant surprise." He hugged his daughter. "What brings you by this time of evening?"

"Is Mom around? There's something I need to talk to you both about."

"She's not here, but she's just downstairs at her friend's house. It's bridge night or pinochle or canasta or whatever that card game is she plays." Albert moved to pick up the phone. "I'll call her and get her up here if you'd like."

Ivy nodded. "Please do. It's kinda important."

Albert studied her as he dialed the number. "I hope nothing's wrong."

"No, sir. Everything's going to be all right."

He furrowed his brow in confusion. "What does that mean?" His attention was diverted when his call was answered. He spoke for a minute or so on the phone, then hung up and turned to Ivy.

"Your mother will be right up. Want to give me any hints?"

Ivy shook her head. "It won't be long now—just wait."

Albert made a face but resigned himself to being patient. Ivy entered the living room and made herself comfortable on the sofa. Albert sat across from her in a wing chair. They had only waited a few minutes when Grace burst into the room.

"What's going on? Is everything OK?" She was slightly flushed and out of breath.

"Mom! Did you run all the way up here?"

Grace shook her head. "Certainly not. Just all the way from the elevator. Now never mind that. What's going on?"

"Mom, you're going to want to have a seat." Ivy patted the sofa next to her.

"OK, now you're scaring me," Grace said as she settled on the sofa.

"There's nothing to be afraid of," Ivy assured them. "I've got some news. I think it's good news, and I hope you will, too."

"Just out with it, Ivy," Albert demanded. "I've been patient long enough."

Ivy took a deep breath and began. "Mom, Dad— I'm pregnant. I'll be having a baby in March."

For one electric moment, nobody in the room moved or spoke. Then suddenly the bubble burst and Albert and Grace started talking at once.

"A baby! Honey, that's wonderful." Albert sprang out of his chair to hug his daughter.

"A baby? Honey, how are you going to do that?" Grace looked at her in stunned disbelief.

Ivy took a moment to sort out her parents' reactions. Once Albert released her, she turned to her mother. "What do you mean, how am I going to do that? Do what?"

"Have a baby—raise a child on your own?" Grace suddenly perked up. "Wait a minute—does this mean you and Keith are getting back together?"

Ivy was speechless.

"You and Keith. He is the father, right? Oh, this is wonderful news." Grace clapped her hands happily.

"Hold up, Mom. This doesn't have anything to do with Keith. Well, OK," she corrected, "it does have *something* to do with Keith. But we're not getting back together. I told him he could be as involved or uninvolved as he chose to be. This is my decision, and I'm going to have this baby regardless of what Keith does or doesn't do."

"But Ivy, you can't be planning to raise this child on your own." Grace looked shocked.

"I'm not going to be on my own . . . I'll have your help, won't I?"

Grace nodded quickly. "Yes, of course, but a baby needs both of its parents. You can't deprive your child of its God-given right to be loved and nurtured by a mother and a father."

Ivy studied her mother carefully. "Mom, what are you saying?"

"I'm saying I have believed all along that not marrying Keith was a big mistake. And this happy news just reaffirms my convictions." Grace grasped Ivy's hands. "Baby, you have to reconsider your decision about Keith—if not for yourself, then for your baby. It's the right thing to do."

"I have amazing news!"

Just as Ivy had suspected, Keith left Navy Pier

and immediately began calling everyone he could think of to spread the word.

"Keith!" The feminine voice registered delight. "This is a pleasant surprise. I didn't expect to hear from you until this weekend."

"Well, I just heard some wonderful news and I couldn't wait to share it with you."

"Do tell."

"Ivy's pregnant! She's having my baby!"

The line hummed as stony silence met his announcement.

"When did you find out?" she asked finally.

"Tonight. She met me after work and told me." Keith paused for a moment. "You don't seem especially surprised."

"Oh, trust me," the woman said dryly. "I'm surprised." She fell silent again.

"Are you there? Say something." Keith demanded.

"What do you want me to say? Congratulations? That hardly seems to be the right response."

"Why not? This is excellent news." Keith's enthusiasm was unbridled. "Don't you see, Ivy will have to come back to me now—we're having a child together. I will make her see that our baby needs both of its parents."

"Keith," the woman said impatiently, "even if that were true, and in my mind that's a mighty big *if,* why would that be good news for me?"

"Oh, you're not going to start that again, are you? We're just friends, remember?"

"Friends who have sex," she interjected.

"Well, yeah." Keith seemed genuinely confused by her reaction. "And as friends, we want what's best for each other—right? I believe, I have always believed, that Ivy is what's best for me."

"And I have never shared that belief with you. What about that other guy—Ben something? How do you even know this is your baby?"

"I know because she is eight weeks along, and eight weeks ago we were closer than we'd ever been." Keith took a deep breath. "And I know because Ivy is not the kind of woman to sneak around and cheat. She's got more integrity than that."

"What are you trying to say, Keith? You wouldn't be questioning *my* integrity, would you?" Unexpectedly, the woman laughed. "Talk about the pot calling the kettle black!"

"I know you have enough integrity to step back and let Ivy and me work this out—without any interference." Keith's voice grew stern. "And I know I can count on your continued discretion."

The laughter continued, the sound teetering between maniacal and hysterical. "What you can count on, Keith," she managed between breaths, "is that I'm going to stand back and watch you fall on your face. And when you do, I may or may not be there to pick up the pieces."

"You're wrong," Keith said angrily. "This baby is just the glue Ivy and I need to stick together. You'll see." He slammed down the phone, anxious to escape the laughter.

Ivy left her parents' house, her mind reeling from her mother's words: *Reconsider—if not for yourself, then for your baby.*

Driving to her apartment, she questioned the choices she'd made up to this point. "What do I owe my child?" Her voice filled the car, but no answer came. Instinctively she knew her destiny lay in the answer to that question.

Seventeen

During the next few days Ivy fended off questions and lived in the eye of the storm created by her news. Her friends each reacted much as she expected: Kim was excited; Cherise was disappointed; Trina and Danielle were surprised; but all her friends were supportive and committed to helping Ivy in any way they could.

Grace and Albert were thrilled, already planning how they would spoil their first grandchild. Ivy had even received congratulations from Keith's parents. Keith was quickly reestablishing himself as a regular fixture in her life. Once he recovered from his initial shock, he was attentive and solicitous—almost too much for Ivy's taste. She wanted him to back off and give her room to think, but that seemed to be the last thing on Keith's agenda. It was all very overwhelming to Ivy. And one aspect of her life remained very much unresolved.

She had decided that she wanted to tell Ben her news face-to-face, so all she could do was wait until he returned. She had replied to his letter, but in terms so general and statements so platonic that it could have been a letter written to a distant relative. The words from his letter still burned in her heart, but she didn't think it would be fair of her to hint of a relationship that could not be—not now, while another man's child grew in her belly.

Ivy received another letter from Ben, this one much more reserved and tentative than before. In it, he spoke of his job, the people, and the countryside, but he wrote nothing of a personal nature.

As she read his letter, Ivy felt tears well up in the corners of her eyes. *I haven't even told him,* she thought, *and I've lost him already.*

The weeks passed slowly, but they did pass. Finally, it was time for Ben to come home. Ivy knew what day he was due to return, but she didn't know exactly what time. It saddened her to realize that if their relationship had progressed along the path it had seemed to be taking when he left, she would most likely have been meeting him at the airport. As it was, all she could do on that Friday night was wait by the phone for his call. The call didn't come until the next afternoon.

"Hello?" Ivy answered on the first ring.

"Hey, Ivy. It's Ben."

Waves of relieved happiness washed over Ivy at the sound of his voice. She tossed aside the baby magazine she had been trying to read and focused on the phone. "Oh, Ben," she breathed. "Welcome home! I was hoping to hear from you yesterday."

"I'm sorry. The plane didn't get in until late, and by the time I'd cleared Customs and gotten home, it was even later and I didn't want to wake you."

"It would have been OK," she assured him. "I've

been waiting to talk to you. I've missed you," she added.

"I missed you, too," Ben seemed to perk up. "I brought you something back. I can't wait to give it to you."

"Then don't wait. Come on over."

"If you're sure this is a good time," Ben said hesitantly.

"Of course I'm sure. I'm really anxious to see you." Ivy picked her next words carefully. "We have a lot of catching up to do."

"I'll be there within the hour."

They said their good-byes and the call ended. Ivy sat back on the sofa and chewed her bottom lip nervously. *How do I tell you, Ben? And what's going to happen when I do? Will you turn away from me completely?* Ivy's heart began to hurt as she considered that possibility. Ben's friendship was something she had come to count on. The thought of losing even that filled her with unspeakable sadness.

Maybe I don't have to tell him yet, a voice in her head chimed hopefully. *I'm not showing yet . . . it could be my secret for a while longer if I wanted it to be.*

Ivy shook her head, rejecting that idea before it had a chance to take root. "I have to tell him—now, today. I owe him that much. I decided when I chose to have this baby to let the chips fall where they may, and that's what I'm going to do." Sounding more resolute than she felt, Ivy scooted off the couch and headed back to the bedroom to change. Even though she was not showing any significant signs of the pregnancy yet, she wanted to put on something a little more loose than the T-shirt and shorts she was wearing.

She was in her bathroom checking her appearance one more time when the door buzzer sounded. *Here goes nothing* . . . She took a deep cleansing breath and hurried to admit her guest. She opened her apartment door and went out to stand at the top of the steps to greet Ben. It was all she could do not to leap into his arms when he approached her apartment. As it was, she hopped impatiently from one foot to the other waiting for him to reach her. For his part, Ben took the stairs two at a time, hurrying to be near her. Then he reached her, and all the weeks of separation and feelings of uncertainty fell away as they wrapped each other in a smothering embrace.

"I really missed you," he whispered into her ear. "It feels so good to hold you again."

Ben's words were like a bucket of cold water being poured over Ivy's head. *I have to be fair to him,* she thought. *He has to know the truth.* She gently eased out of the hug.

"It's good to see you, too," she said lamely.

Ben studied her closely, wondering about the sudden change in her demeanor. "You look wonderful," he ventured. "A real sight for sore eyes."

Ivy's smile was genuine. "You're looking good, too. Africa must agree with you." It was true. The weeks of relatively primitive conditions had honed Ben's physique, making him lean and more prominently muscled. The sun had tanned his honey-colored skin a deeper, richer shade. And he'd grown a beard.

Despite her intentions, Ivy reached out and rubbed his chin. "This is new."

Ben laughed. "Shaving didn't seem so important in the village. It was just easier to let it grow. But I plan to shave it all off now that I'm home."

Sensual images of Ben's beard scratching against her skin ran through Ivy's mind, but she kept the thoughts to herself. Pushing the intimate visions away, Ivy moved to safer ground.

"Come in." She stepped aside to allow him entry. "I want to hear all about your trip."

Ben again noticed her change in attitude, but again decided to let it pass. *Something's going on,* he thought, more convinced than ever. *But she'll tell me when she's ready.*

He entered the apartment and turned to face her. "I have something for you." He held out a shopping bag.

Smiling broadly, she accepted the bag and looked inside. "Oh, Ben," she breathed, "it's beautiful." She reached in the bag and pulled out several yards of vibrantly colored woven cloth. The reds, yellows, greens, and blues formed an intricate diamond pattern that repeated throughout the length of the cloth.

"I got it at the market outside the village," he explained. "The woman who sold it to me wove it herself. I thought you would look beautiful in those colors."

Ivy hugged him again. "Thank you so much. I'm going to have this made into a dress. You were so sweet to think of me."

"Look in the bag," Ben directed. "There's something else."

She looked again and pulled out a necklace consisting of a single cowrie shell strung on a braided leather cord.

"Cowrie shells symbolize prosperity," Ben said. "It is my wish for you."

"I love it!" she exclaimed. "Will you put it on me?" She handed him the necklace and turned her back to him.

Ben slid the necklace in place. As he fastened the knotted closure, his fingers brushed against her neck. That briefest and most innocent of touches sent small tremors through both of them. Ivy quickly moved away.

"Thank you again. I really love my gifts." She motioned to the sofa. "Now sit down and tell me all about your trip."

Ben studied her carefully, trying to discern what was different between them. After a moment, he shrugged and settled on her sofa.

"Liberia was like nothing I've ever experienced before," he began.

The next half hour passed pleasantly enough, with Ben regaling Ivy with stories of life in Liberia. Soon, however, Ben's tales ended and an uncomfortable silence developed between them. Ivy took a deep breath to gather her courage. She looked deeply into Ben's eyes and began.

"I have something to tell you."

"I think I know."

"You do?" Her face scrunched in question.

"It's about Keith, right? You two reconciled while

I was away." Ben's eyes mirrored his sadness. "I figured that had happened when I got your letter. You didn't even mention our night together—I took that to mean you were trying to forget it."

"It's not what you think," Ivy began. "It's so much more than just a reconciliation."

Ben's brow furrowed. "What does that mean? What are you saying?"

Ivy took a deep, steadying breath. "I wish there was some easy way to say this, but there isn't, believe me. I've been trying to find the right words for weeks now."

Ben said nothing; he just looked intently at her, a sense of dread filling his soul.

"Ben, I'm pregnant. Almost three months along now."

After feeling an initial shock, Ben did some quick calculations in his head. "That means that Keith . . ."

"Yes," Ivy confirmed. "Keith is my baby's father."

"So I was right—you and Keith are getting back together." His words carried an edge of finality.

"I haven't made that decision yet," she said. "It was hard enough to decide to have the baby. I'm just taking each day at a time. I don't know what the future will hold, but I do know that I'm going to love and care for this baby no matter what else happens."

Ben nodded. "Of course you will. You're going to be a wonderful mother." He grew quiet and pensive. "I knew from your letters something was up," he said finally. "I had no idea this was it, but

I knew it was something." He rose and started for the door.

"Are you leaving?" Ivy's eyes widened.

"Yes, I think it's best." He turned to face her. "Ivy, I want what's best for you and your child. Please know, I have always been, and I will continue to be, your friend. Nothing you've said here could change that."

"And yet you're leaving." The tears she had tried to keep at bay slipped down her cheeks.

"Just for now," he smiled weakly. "You've dropped a bombshell on me. I need time to process it."

Ivy nodded her understanding. "Call me later?"

Ben nodded. "Count on it." He gave her one last soulful look and then closed the door gently as he left.

Woodenly, on legs that didn't feel like his own, Ben lurched down the stairs and out of Ivy's apartment building. His mind was reeling and his heart was aching. Somehow, he managed to get into his car before he fell apart. Inside the relative privacy of his car, Ben rested his forehead against the steering wheel and allowed the shock and pain that had hovered around the edges of his consciousness to consume him completely.

Pregnant . . . I knew things were going too well. I just knew that other shoe had to drop. Just when I thought all the pieces of my happiness were falling into place—just when I thought I had found the One. Pregnant . . .

Ben lifted his head and rubbed his eyes as if trying to clear away an unpleasant sight. He sat quietly for a moment longer, considering his next move. Suddenly, he knew exactly whose viewpoint he wanted to hear. Starting the engine, he eased the car away from the curb and pointed it in the direction of his sister's home.

A short time later, he was ringing the doorbell of Dionne's East Side Chicago home.

"Ben!" Dionne rushed out and wrapped him in a bear hug. "What a wonderful surprise! I didn't expect to see you until breakfast tomorrow."

"It's good to see you, too, sis." Ben returned the hug. "I really need to talk to you—and I wanted to do it in private, without the clan around."

"Sounds serious." Dionne released him and pulled him inside the house. "Come sit down and talk to me."

Ben entered her small but comfortable brick bungalow.

"Kids home?" he asked as he paced the living room.

"No," Dionne said, watching him closely. "They're actually out at Mom's house. They wanted to spend the night with her to help her get ready for Uncle Ben's big homecoming breakfast."

Ben grimaced. "You know how much I hate being called *Uncle* Ben."

Dionne laughed. "Well, little bro, you are what you are." She took a seat on the sofa. "Now suppose you tell me what's up. You're obviously upset about something. What it is I can't imagine, since you just got back in town."

"Yeah . . . you wouldn't think things could go so wrong so fast, would you?"

"Bennie, what's going on?" Dionne prompted again.

Ben stopped his aimless trek across her living room. "Dionne, I need some advice. It's about my friend Ivy."

Dionne nodded her head knowingly. "I figured it had to do with some woman. But she has to be more than a friend to have you this upset. OK, spit it out."

So he did. Dionne became the first person in Ben's family to hear the entire story about Ivy, beginning at the moment he rescued her on the El train to the moment he stumbled out of her apartment reeling from the news of her pregnancy.

Once he finished, Dionne fell back against the sofa cushion, shaking her head. "Bennie, what have you gotten yourself into?" she muttered. "I'm not sure what you want me to say. You want my advice about what? You can't be considering pursuing a relationship with this woman, can you?"

Ben's face fell. "Why do you say that?"

Dionne looked stunned. "Bennie! You said it yourself when you told me the story. You said, *I knew she had a lot of baggage to begin with*. Bennie, girlfriend's baggage just became a steamer trunk. She's having somebody else's baby. You can't get involved with that."

"But I'm already involved," Ben said. "I'm already in too deep to back out now."

"Bennie, you don't have any choice. You are not that baby's father. And from what you say, the father is still in the picture."

"But she doesn't love him," Ben was quick to

protest. "If she had loved him she would have married him and we would never have met."

"That was then," Dionne said firmly, "and this is now. Having a child together ties two people for life. That baby deserves to have both of its parents. You can't get in the middle of that."

Ben rolled his eyes in disgust. "Dionne! Could you really be arguing for Ivy to stay with the father for the sake of the baby? Do you actually think that's a good idea?"

"What I think is that that baby deserves a family. And I think you shouldn't interfere with that. Did you ask this woman—"

"Ivy," Ben interjected angrily. "Her name is Ivy."

"Whatever." Dionne waved dismissively. "Did you ask *Ivy* if she and the baby's father were getting back together?"

"She said she wasn't sure," he mumbled, looking away from his sister's scrutiny.

"She's not sure." Dionne shook her head sagely. "The writing's on the wall, Bennie. I'll bet you dollars to donuts that Ivy and her baby's daddy will be back together before the baby turns a year old. And you'll be standing around with your heart in your hands if you don't walk away now. You need to get while the getting's good."

Ben snorted. "You know, Dee, I came to you because I figured you'd be the one person in the family who might understand. The one person who would understand how destructive it is for people to stay together for the sake of the kids."

"I do understand," she assured him. "But I know how hard it is to raise a child alone. And I know that even under the best of circumstances, being a single mother is far more difficult than having two loving parents in the home. Step back, Bennie. Let Ivy's baby have the family every baby is entitled to."

"You're starting to sound just like Momma."

Dionne laughed lightly. "Well, what can I say—I'm Judy's daughter."

"That you are, Dee." Ben bent down to kiss her forehead. "That you are." He started toward the door.

"Wait . . ." Dionne quickly rose to follow him. "You aren't leaving yet, are you? We haven't even talked about your trip."

"In the morning at breakfast, Dee. You'll hear all about it then." Ben opened the door. "Right now I'm tired and I have a lot of thinking to do." He started out the door. "Oh, and one more thing," he turned back to face her. "Don't say anything about Ivy to the rest of the family. I want to handle it my way."

Dionne nodded. "Of course, Bennie. But I've got to say it again—there's nothing for you to handle. Just back away, while you still can."

"That's just it, Dee. I think it's already too late." Ben walked out the door.

Sunday morning breakfast was a joyous, noisy gathering. Ben was very nearly suffocated by the hugs and kisses showered on him by family. His mother kept touching him, rubbing his shoulders or caressing his cheek, as if to reassure herself that he was really there.

Ben's time in Liberia was the sole subject of conversation around the breakfast table. His nephews, Dionne's children, kept peppering Ben with questions about the village and the children. Anthony, the older child, was both fascinated and appalled by the fact that the African children were in school during what he felt should have been summer vacation.

After the breakfast dishes were cleared away, Ben pulled out the presents. Squealing with delight, the children ran off to play with their carved wooden animal figurines.

Tracy and Dionne were awed by the intricate design on the woven bags their brother gave them. Greg declared he couldn't wait to get into his garden with the handmade tools. And Judy's eyes filled with tears when she saw the magnificent caftan with its matching headdress.

"I'm going to look like a queen in this," she exclaimed.

"That's exactly why I bought it," Ben nodded. "Because you are certainly queen of this tribe. I figured you needed an outfit to dress the part."

Ben smiled, pleased that his presents had been so well received. He also felt a sense of relief that he'd made it through the entire breakfast without having to talk about or even think about the situation with Ivy. True to her word, Dionne had not said anything to the family, but that did not stop her from shooting highly charged looks at Ben periodically throughout the morning.

The breakfast gathering lasted longer than was customary, but eventually the Stephens family began to disperse. Dionne and the children left first, hurrying to get to Anthony's Little League game. Tracy was next, on her way to the movies with a friend. Greg emerged from the back of the house carrying his golf clubs over his shoulder. After accepting the good luck wished to him by his wife and son, Greg headed out to conquer the links.

Judy watched her husband disappear through the garage door and then turned to her son.

"OK, you ready to tell me about it now?"

Ben feigned confusion. "Tell you about what?"

"Don't give me that, Benjamin J. Stephens. There is something bothering you . . . has been since you walked in the door." She wagged her finger at him. "And don't think I didn't notice all those looks your sister kept giving you. I assumed you didn't want to talk about it in front of the whole family, but now it's just you and me. So out with it."

"What are you, Mom—one of the psychic friends?" Ben tried to laugh it off.

"You better believe I am when it comes to my kids. Now come on, tell me what's bothering you."

Ben hesitated. He knew in his heart that his mother would not rest until he'd told her what was going on. So although he was relatively sure how she would respond, he gave in.

"Have a seat, Momma. I'll try to make a long story short."

Judy listened intently as Ben laid out the situation with Ivy. He told her everything except that he and Ivy had made love. Some things were better left unsaid, he decided. When he told Judy about Dionne's response, she nodded.

"I think your sister's right about you backing off, but not for the reasons she said. I agree with you, it's a bad move for anybody to stay together for the sake of a baby. But I agree with Dionne that nothing good can come of this for you. You're going to get your heart broken, and as your mother who loves you, I can't stand idly by and watch that happen." Concern shone in Judy's eyes. "This Ivy will reconcile with her baby's father, and even though I don't think it will last, that doesn't mean I think you ought to be around, waiting to pick up the pieces. There's nothing in it for you, Ben. Nothing but heartache and pain."

Back in his apartment, Ben sat quietly reflecting on the advice given to him by his mother and sister. Intellectually, he knew they were probably right; he knew he should cut his losses with Ivy and move on. But in his heart, he knew he wasn't ready to do that.

"I don't know what's going to happen," his voice echoed in the quiet apartment, "but I know I want Ivy in my life."

Several days passed as Ben readjusted to his life in Chicago. During that time, the situation with Ivy was never very far from his mind. Finally, he made the only decision he thought he had. One evening about a week after he'd learned the news, Ben called Ivy to see if he could stop by. She readily agreed.

"Have a seat," she invited when he arrived.

"No," Ben fidgeted restlessly near the door. "I won't be staying long. There's something I need to say to you."

Ivy closed the door and turned to face him. "I'm listening."

Ben took a deep breath. "I have been thinking about your news ever since you told me. In fact, I have thought of little else. I didn't know what to do or how to feel. But after much consideration, I have made a decision." He took a step toward her. "I have been and I will continue to be your friend. I will be here for whatever you need, whenever you need it. All you have to do is ask." Ben reached out to caress her cheek and looked deeply into her eyes. "But that's all I can be. I have come to believe that you and Keith and your baby should be a family. I can't interfere with that."

Ivy could not manage words, choosing instead to nuzzle the warm hand that stroked her cheek.

"I'll never be more than a phone call away," he said softly.

"You promise?" she whispered, fighting against the threatening tears.

"I promise." He partially surrendered to his longing and brushed her lips with a feather-light kiss. "I'd better go now."

Ivy's sadness mounted as she watched him open the door and hurry out of the apartment. The

door closed behind him solidly, filling Ivy with a
sense of finality that nearly overwhelmed her.

"So that's it," she murmured. "The man I want
only wants to be my friend, and the man I don't
want is the father of my unborn child." She shook
her head slowly. "When did my life get to be such
a mess?"

Eighteen

"OK ladies, pick your focal point and concentrate." The instructor's voice rose above the din as she walked among the couples on pallets on the floor. "Focus and breathe through your mouth with short, panting breaths."

Ivy tried not to think about how ridiculous she must look and sound, crouched over and panting like a dog. Since the instructor had assured Ivy and her Lamaze classmates that doing this would help ease the pain of labor, Ivy was willing to extend the benefit of the doubt.

"You're doing great, Ivy." Keith rubbed her lower back as the instructor had directed the Lamaze coaches to do.

Ivy chuckled and made a face. "This is the easy part," she said. "Let's see how I do when it's the real thing."

"You'll be fine," Keith assured her. "And I'll be right there with you, coaching you on."

Ivy twisted slightly to look at him. "Oh, I have no doubts that you'll be there."

She returned to her Lamaze breathing but instead of a focal point, Ivy's thoughts wandered back to when Keith first asked her about joining a class.

* * *

"Oh, I don't know, Keith. I hadn't given it any thought." Ivy had barely glanced at the brochure Keith held out to her.

"It's time to think about it," Keith insisted. "We're in the eighth month. These childbirth classes fill up fast, and I want to be sure we get in the right one."

"We're in the eighth month?" Ivy's lip curled.

Ivy's pregnancy had progressed in textbook-perfect fashion. Physically, she had had no problems. After the initial morning sickness had passed, Ivy had maintained her active lifestyle, gained a normal amount of weight, and passed each checkup with flying colors.

Emotionally, things in her life were not nearly as picture perfect. Keith was determined to be a part of the pregnancy. Under normal circumstances, Ivy supposed she would be grateful for the support, but these were not normal circumstances. As it was, his attention grated on her. And the fact that everyone around her, Ben included, seemed to think that Keith's involvement was a good thing, irritated her even more.

It's just that my hormones are out of control, she often rationalized internally when she found herself annoyed by Keith. *How many thousands of women would give their left arm to have this kind of help and support?*

But her personal pep talks did nothing to ease her irritation. So far she had managed to keep her true feelings from Keith. He either didn't know or didn't care that she secretly wanted him to leave her alone.

"C'mon, Ivy. Look at the brochure again." Keith's voice had drawn her back to the issue at hand. "A woman in my office told me this place has the best childbirth classes in town. But they fill up fast. It might be too late. We probably should have registered as soon as we found out we were pregnant."

"When *we* found out *we* were pregnant? Please Keith, give me a break," Ivy snapped. "*We* are not pregnant—*I* am. And I'll decide if and when and where I want to go to childbirth classes."

"Of course you can decide." Keith's tone was slightly condescending. "It's just that everybody I've talked to says it's very important to go to these classes, so I would hope you decide to participate in one—for the sake of the baby."

Ivy rolled her eyes. "I have just about had it with you telling me to do things or not do things or eat things or not eat things for the sake of the baby. Don't think I don't know you're using this baby to try and control me."

Keith reared back as if he'd been slapped. "You're overwrought, and I know you aren't thinking about what you're saying. I know you know that I would never try to control you. I'm just trying to make sure that everything is perfect. I only want the best for my family."

Ivy sighed. "I'm not your family, Keith." She snatched the brochure from his hand. "Let me look it over, and I'll decide what I want to do."

"Sure, Ivy. Whatever you want." Keith's tone was

the vocal equivalent to a pat on the head. "Just let me know when and where."

Why do you just assume you'll be my birthing partner? The words screamed through Ivy's mind, but she held her tongue. "It's getting late," she said instead. "Shouldn't you be leaving?"

Keith checked his watch. "You're right. I do have to run." He kissed his fingertips and pressed them against Ivy's belly. "Bye-bye, baby. Daddy'll see you soon." He kissed Ivy's cheek. "Bye-bye, baby. Daddy'll see you soon, too."

Ivy gritted her teeth and again said nothing, instead mentally urging him to leave. When he finally did close the apartment door behind him, Ivy let out a huge sigh of relief. She knew Keith was right—a Lamaze class would be a smart thing to do for herself and her baby—but she wasn't ready to admit it. She found herself resisting the idea just because it came from Keith.

"That's silly and unfair," she declared. "Keith is trying to be helpful and involved. I shouldn't push him away." She listened to the sound of the words, tested the feel of them. And then she made a decision. "I'm through fighting this. It takes too much energy, and it can't be good for me or the baby. If Keith wants to participate, so be it. I'll take all the help I can get."

She thought for a moment about all the help she had. Her parents and Keith's were all very solicitous, calling and checking on her regularly. Her friends were all supportive in varying degrees. Kim and Trina were constantly playing mother hen, while Danielle and Cherise, who had both questioned the wisdom of the pregnancy to begin with, were helpful but a bit more reserved. Either would do anything Ivy asked, but neither volunteered very often. Ivy accepted their reactions without question.

Ben's reaction, however, was a source of almost constant confusion for her. Once Ben had decided he could only be her friend, he was steadfast in that decision. The things they once did together, such as lunches and movies, were things of the past. Initially she had asked him why they couldn't still have lunch, since friends had lunch all the time. Ben had shaken his head and given a vague excuse that Ivy hadn't believed but had accepted. Once school started in the fall, lunch was out of the question since it was difficult for him to get away during the day.

He was still very helpful, offering to pick up groceries or run errands for her. But he had obviously set boundaries for their friendship—boundaries that he was not going to cross or even reveal.

About the same time Ivy decided to stop trying to fight Keith's involvement, she decided to stop trying to force Ben's. She still talked to Ben once a week or so, but she had not suggested they get together again, and neither had he. His withdrawal saddened her, but she was making her peace with it.

"OK, moms and coaches, that's it for today." The Lamaze instructor's voice brought Ivy back to the present. "I'll see you next week." The instructor smiled. "Unless you have your baby before then." Nervous laughter met that quip.

Keith helped Ivy up from the pallet. She struggled to her feet with great difficulty.

"I'm as big as a barn," she complained. "I feel like Gracie the elephant."

"You look beautiful. You're positively glowing," Keith said.

"Glow my eye," she retorted. "That's sweat. Panting is hard work."

Keith chuckled. "Come on, let me get you home so you can get off your feet."

Once they reached her apartment, Keith helped her get settled. "Do you want me to stay until somebody gets here?"

"Keith, please, just go. I'll be fine. Don't worry."

Keith looked skeptical, although it was obvious he really wanted to go. "Well, if you're sure . . ."

"I'm sure. Go on, and I'll talk to you tomorrow."

Keith kissed her on the forehead and left. And just like that, Ivy found herself unexpectedly alone on a Friday night. Virtually every night since she'd begun her eighth month of pregnancy, someone had been with her. Between her friends, her parents, and Keith, she hadn't had a private night in weeks. But Keith said he had a big business dinner to attend, her parents were attending a play with a group of people from their building, and her friends all had plans for the night. Each of her team of helpers thought someone else would be on the job for the night.

Once Ivy realized how the schedule was going to develop, she was very careful not to let any of them know that she was going to be alone.

I'll be fine, she thought defiantly. *It's just one night, and goodness knows I deserve a little peace and quiet.*

So after fending off the calls from everyone checking in with her, Ivy turned the ringer off on the phone and ran a steaming hot bubble bath. It was against her doctor's advice—Ivy was supposed to take only showers at this point in the pregnancy—but as she undressed and put on her thick chenille robe, Ivy decided that one long, soaking bath would not hurt anything.

She's just worried about me getting in and out of the tub, Ivy thought as she poured some gardenia-scented oil into the tub. *But I'll be very careful.* An idea hit her. She lumbered into the dining room and got one of her wood dinette chairs. Dragging the chair back to the bathroom, Ivy put it right next to the tub.

"There," she said. "I'll use that to help me get in and out." Problem solved, she went to her bedroom to get a good book. After selecting a paperback romance novel, she draped her robe on the back of the chair and eased her way into the tub.

"Ahhhh . . ." A deep sigh of satisfaction escaped from Ivy as the warm scented water closed over her large body. "At last." She lay back in the tub and opened her book. She had been reading for only a few minutes when the first twinge of pain hit.

At first she ignored it. The pain wasn't that bad; she had been having false contractions for days, and her due date was still two weeks away. She rubbed absently at the spot of the pain, shifted in the tub, and kept reading.

About half an hour had passed before the second pain hit. This one demanded more attention.

"Damn," Ivy gasped. She tossed the book to the floor and reached for the seat of the chair, sloshing water on the floor as she went. Using the chair to get out of the tub proved much more challenging than using it to get in. Between the water, the bubbles, and the oil, Ivy had to exercise extreme caution to avoid slipping and falling.

A bath seemed like a good idea an hour ago, she thought ruefully. *Now, not so much.* She eased back into the tub and hit the drain release lever with her toe. She waited as the water drained from the tub. When she was sitting in an empty tub, she tried the chair maneuver again. This time she managed to hoist herself to her knees, and using the chair for balance, she stood and stepped out of the tub. A smug smile spread across her face. "See," she muttered. "I knew I could do it."

The third pain snatched the smile right off her face. Grabbing a towel and her robe, Ivy made her way to the bedroom and the phone on her nightstand. She reached for her list of phone and pager numbers. She tried Keith's cell phone first.

"The cellular phone you are calling is either turned off or out of the service area."

Ivy slammed down the phone when she heard the recorded message. Moving on down her list, she tried the cell phone numbers for Kim, Cherise, and Danielle, each time getting either the same recorded message or a voicemail greeting. Since her doctor had warned her that labor could last a very long time, Ivy wasn't worried about getting to the hospital in time. More annoyed than panicked, Ivy decided to get dressed and try the numbers again. She quickly put on one of her loose-fitting maternity dresses and checked her suitcase. Her mother had packed it weeks ago, a move for which Ivy was now very grateful.

Then the fourth pain came and Ivy cried out. Remembering her Lamaze classes, Ivy blew short breaths through her teeth until the pain subsided. When the pain had passed, she checked the clock on her nightstand.

Twenty minutes! They're getting closer together. She tried again to reach Keith's cell phone, and again got the recorded message. She dialed his pager number and punched in her number. She stopped short of adding 911 to her numeric message. *It's not an emergency yet, and I don't want to panic him. I'm sure I still have plenty of time.*

She knew her parents were out of reach—they may have gotten a computer, but a cellular phone was a little too much technology for them. She was waiting for Keith to answer her page when the fifth pain hit—harder than any she had experienced so far. This time Ivy doubled over in pain. She struggled to find a focal point and breathe as she'd been taught. A wave of nausea washed over her as the contraction continued.

When the pain passed, the beginnings of panic closed in on Ivy. *I'm alone, I can't reach anybody, and now the contractions are fifteen minutes apart. This is all happening too fast.*

She considered calling an ambulance and going to the hospital by herself, but she desperately didn't want to give birth alone. Suddenly Ben's voice filled her head: *I will be here for whatever you need, whenever you need it. All you have to do is ask. I'm only a phone call away.*

It took her only a moment to decide.

Please be there, she prayed as she dialed.

"Hello?" Ben answered on the third ring.

"Oh, thank God! Ben, I need you."

"Ivy?" Ben's voice revealed his surprise. "Is that you?"

"Yes, it's me, and I need you now."

"What is it? What's wrong?" His surprise was quickly replaced with concern.

Just then, another contraction hit her. "Having baby . . . now . . ." she managed between breaths. "Need . . . you."

"I'm on my way." Ben hung up the phone and grabbed his keys as he raced out the door. He covered the distance between their apartments in record time, disregarding all traffic laws and driving with reckless abandon.

When he reached her building, he double-parked in front and ran up the sidewalk to the stoop. He pressed the intercom button insistently, as if pressing the button multiple times would make the door open on its own.

"Ben, hurry." Ivy's voice came through the intercom seconds before the buzzer sounded, unlocking the door. Ben snatched the door open and took the stairs two at a time. Ivy met him at her apartment door with her suitcase in her hand.

"Thank you so much for coming to get me." Her voice was weak and thready.

"Of course I'd come to get you. Which hospital?"

She told him, and he nodded. He took her suitcase and pulled her door closed. After wrapping her arm around his shoulders, Ben guided Ivy down the stairs and out to his car.

With just as much speed as before, but more regard for public safety, Ben raced through Chicago to get Ivy to the hospital. Ivy had called ahead, so there was an orderly with a wheelchair waiting for her at the hospital's maternity entrance.

"Go on and park your car, Dad," the orderly told Ben. "I'll take Mom on up. You can meet her on the third floor."

Ben opened his mouth to protest, "I'm not the father," but the orderly whisked Ivy away before he had the chance.

After Ben finally found a parking space, he hurried to the third floor nurses' station.

"I'm looking for Ivy Daniels," he told the nurse on duty.

"Oh, good. You're here." The nurse handed Ben a hospital scrub outfit. "You need to put this on first, Dad, and then I'll take you to her. You can change in that dressing room down the hall. There's a bag in there to put your clothes in." She pointed at a door a few feet away.

"But I'm not—" Ben began.

"You need to hurry, Dad." The nurse interrupted. "Her labor is progressing very quickly." The nurse grabbed Ben's arm and turned him in the direction of the dressing room. Ben hesitated, feeling very much like a deer caught in the glare of oncoming headlights.

"Go on," the nurse urged. "There's not a lot of time."

Shrugging, Ben hurried to the dressing room to change. When he emerged minutes later, the nurse was waiting for him.

"This way," she pushed him gently. "She's in here."

When Ben entered the labor room, he saw that Ivy was hooked up to various monitors, all of which were beeping loudly. Ivy was concentrating on her breathing, trying to control the pain of another contraction.

"That's it," a nurse who was watching the monitors encouraged. "You're doing fine."

Ivy looked up when Ben entered. She held out her hand to him. Slowly, Ben crossed the room and took her hand.

"I'm sorry, Ben. I know this isn't what you had in mind when you offered to do whatever I needed."

Ben shook his head. "Don't apologize. I'm just glad I can be here for you. But Ivy, where's Keith? Shouldn't he be here?"

Ivy shook her head. "I don't know where he is. I called his cell phone and paged him, but the contractions started coming too fast and I was afraid to try and wait for him to get back with me. Hopefully he'll know to get here as soon as he can."

"So you called me." Ben smiled. "I'm really glad you did. But I have no idea what I'm doing."

Ivy managed a weak smile. "Well, neither do I. But I imagine the baby'll be born whether we know what to do or not."

The nurse who had been watching the monitors came over to him. "It's very easy," she said. "Your job as coach is just to be here for Mom, encourage her, rub her back if she needs it, and feed her ice chips if she gets thirsty. Nature will take care of the rest."

Ben nodded gratefully. "Sounds like a job I can handle."

"Here we go again," Ivy muttered. Ben turned to her as she gripped his hand hard. He held her as she struggled through the contraction. When it passed, Ivy fell back against the pillows, exhausted.

"That one was the worst so far," she said.

"Let me check." The nurse slipped on gloves, guided Ivy's legs into the stirrups, and checked her cervix.

"Almost time to push. I'll go get your doctor." The nurse hurried out of the room, leaving Ben and Ivy alone.

"You ready for this?" she asked.

"I'm not the one who has to be ready," he smiled. "I'm only the ice-chip man. You're the one with the big job."

"Ben, I am really glad you're here." Ivy looked deeply into his eyes. "Thank you for coming to my rescue yet again."

Ben smiled tenderly at her. "All a part of the service, ma'am."

The doctor came in then. "I hear we're just about ready to have a baby," she said cheerfully.

She looked curiously at Ben. "We haven't met; I'm Dr. Jenkins."

Ben shook her extended hand. "I'm Ben, a friend of Ivy's. Apparently, Keith is not available, so the second string was called in."

"Well, Ben, let's get our girl into a delivery room."

Ben followed the gurney as Ivy was wheeled down the hall to a delivery room. Her contractions were right on top of each other; she barely had time to catch her breath in between.

Following Dr. Jenkins's instructions, Ben took his place next to Ivy's shoulder, supporting her in a sitting position. Dr. Jenkins sat on a stool between Ivy's legs, ready to guide the baby out.

"OK, Ivy," Dr. Jenkins said, "with this next contraction I want you to push as hard as you can until I tell you to stop."

Ivy nodded, conserving her breath. The contraction came and Ivy bore down, a guttural moan accompanying the action. Ben held her and muttered words of encouragement as she gripped his hand for strength.

"That was great, Ivy." Dr. Jenkins raised her hand. "Stop for a moment and catch your breath. Now this next contraction should do it. Push with all your strength."

"I can't," Ivy wailed. "I'm tired. I can't push anymore."

"Yes you can," Ben encouraged. "You can do this, Ivy. You're the strongest woman I've ever known. Come on, it's time to meet your baby."

Ivy looked up at Ben, using his expressive eyes

as her focal point. When the wave of pain hit, Ivy pushed with everything within her. Ben tensed, too, as if he could somehow give her some of his strength. After a seemingly interminable time, a loud cry filled the air.

"It's a girl!" Dr. Jenkins gently lifted the tiny infant into the air.

"How is she," Ivy whispered. "Is she OK?"

Ben looked over at the baby and took a quick inventory. "Ten fingers and ten toes. She looks perfect."

Ivy fell back against Ben's arms, exhausted. Dr. Jenkins clamped off the umbilical cord and placed the baby in Ivy's arms. "Here's your daughter, Ivy. Congratulations. She's beautiful."

Ivy looked down into the face of her daughter and felt tears well up in her eyes. Ivy gently touched the soft curls that covered the baby's head. "She *is* beautiful," Ivy said, awed by what she had created. "Happy birthday, princess."

Dr. Jenkins held out a pair of scissors toward Ben. "Would you like to do the honors?" She nodded toward the umbilical cord.

"Oh no, I couldn't," Ben started.

"Ben. You should cut the cord," Ivy insisted. "Please?"

Ben nodded and accepted the scissors from Dr. Jenkins. He took a deep breath and snipped the cord in the space between the two clamps. He looked at Ivy and her baby, an unfamiliar emotion constricting his chest.

One of the nurses gently took the baby from Ivy's arms. "We need to get her cleaned up, and then we'll bring her right back to you." Ivy nodded and blew a kiss at the baby before she was whisked away. Another of the nurses pointed Ben out of the delivery room.

"Go on and change back into your clothes," she said. "The doctor needs to finish up here, and then we'll bring Ivy to her room to recover. You can wait for her there."

Ben nodded and after giving Ivy's hand one last encouraging squeeze, he left the room to change.

Soon he was in a recovery room, waiting for Ivy to be brought in. Ben stood staring out the window, hands shoved in his pockets, deep in thought. He was still shaken and moved by what he and Ivy had experienced together. In the months since he'd returned from Africa, their friendship had waned as he backed away, not wanting to interfere. But when he heard her voice on the phone, it was as if nothing had ever changed between them. But now, having stood by her side as she brought a new life into the world, Ben realized that something had most definitely changed. Even though he wasn't ready to try and say what was different, he instinctively knew something was.

"Here we are, Dad." That same confused orderly from earlier wheeled Ivy into the room. Ben just shook his head and gave up trying to correct the man. Instead he turned his attention to Ivy. He reached for her hand and smoothed a few of the limp twists of hair away from her eyes.

"Hiya, Mom." His voice was low and intimate. "How are you doing?"

Ivy nodded tiredly. "I feel better than I ever have in my life. Did you see the baby?"

"Only for a minute. I haven't seen her since the nurses took her away. Listen, is there anybody you want me to call?"

She shook her head. "For now I just want to rest. Besides, if Keith got the page, he should be here soon. He can call everybody."

A nurse came in then, wheeling a small, see-through bassinet. "Here she is," the nurse spoke in singsong tones. She lifted the baby from the bassinet and placed her in Ivy's arms. "There you go, Mom. This little one is probably hungry. I see from your chart that you're breast-feeding. Are you up to giving it a try?"

Ivy nodded and scooted into a sitting position on the bed. Ben moved back to the window to give her some privacy. A quick breast-feeding lesson later, the nurse left and the sounds of the baby's energetic sucking filled the room.

Ben approached the bed slowly. He was nearly overwhelmed by the simple beauty of the scene laid out before him.

"Oh, Ivy," he whispered, "she's beautiful, just like her mother."

"Thank you." Ivy hesitated for a moment, then said, "Uncle Ben."

Ben laughed at that. "Oh no, let's find something else for her to call me. *Uncle Ben* is not who I want to be. Can't have her growing up thinking I make rice for a living or something."

Their easy laughter mingled into one happy

sound. At that moment Keith burst into the room, breathless and red-faced.

"Ivy! Are you all right? Is the baby OK?" He rushed over to the bed.

"Everything's fine, Keith," Ivy answered. "It's a girl."

"A girl . . . ," Keith breathed. "I have a daughter." Finally Keith noticed Ben. "What the hell are you doing here?" he demanded.

Ben opened his mouth to answer, but Ivy silenced him with a raised hand. "Ben is here because he brought me to the hospital," Ivy said firmly. "I couldn't find you, so I called Ben and he rushed me here. If it hadn't been for Ben, I probably would have had the baby in my bedroom."

"Oh." Immediately, Keith's demeanor changed. He extended his hand. Ben looked at the outstretched hand suspiciously for a moment before accepting the gesture. "Thank you, man," Keith said sincerely as he shook Ben's hand. "I really appreciate what you've done for my family." Keith released Ben and sat on the edge of the bed, ignoring Ben and focusing all his attention on Ivy and the baby.

Dismissed, Ben prepared to leave. Ivy noticed him moving toward the door. "Thank you again, Ben. For everything."

Ben smiled and doffed an imaginary hat. "All a part of the service, ma'am."

Nineteen

Ivy had been home from the hospital for about a week when she called Ben and asked him to come by.

"I haven't seen you since the day the baby was born," she complained. "I'd really like for you to come and visit us."

"How can I say no," Ben smiled. "I'll come by after school."

That afternoon, Ben arrived at Ivy's apartment bearing gifts. When she buzzed him in, she was surprised and pleased to see him.

"Ben, you shouldn't have." She accepted a bouquet of flowers and a brightly wrapped box.

"Of course I should. How better to welcome the prettiest baby girl on the planet?" Ben smiled as he watched Ivy unwrap the present. "I wasn't sure what to get her, so I settled on a schoolteacher kind of gift."

Ivy laughed as she pulled out a set of picture books, crayons, and a child's abacus. "Thanks, Ben. She'll definitely be ready for school."

"I know it's early, but you can never be too prepared." Ben looked around the living room. "So where is the little princess?"

"She's back in the room taking a nap. I'll go get her." Ivy disappeared down the hall, reemerging shortly with the baby wrapped in a powder pink blanket. She offered her bundle to Ben.

"May I?" He seemed hesitant.

"Of course. Sit down and I'll give her to you." After Ben settled on the sofa, Ivy eased the baby into his arms. "Here. Support her head."

"I swear, she's doubled in size since last week. And she's gotten even prettier, if that's possible." Ben looked up at Ivy, who was beaming at him. "You haven't told me her name."

"Rekia Saron," she said proudly.

"Rekia Saron," Ben repeated. "That's positively lyrical. What does it mean?"

"I found it in an African baby name book. Rekia is an Ethiopian name that means *to rise above* and Saron means *joy.*"

Ben nodded. "To rise above . . . that's an interesting choice. Why that?"

"Rekia will face any number of challenges in her life. I want her to be able to rise above them, be bigger than any obstacle that's in her path." Ivy stroked her daughter's hair. "I wanted a name that would give her strength."

"It's a perfect choice," Ben said. "What did Keith say about it?"

Ivy rolled her eyes. "He resisted at first; he wanted to name her something more traditional, but eventually he conceded. My mother almost had a heart attack. Said she was going to die of embarrassment. She swears she is going to call the baby *Ricki,* but I expect she'll come around, too."

"I'll bet she'll be so busy spoiling this baby that she won't have time to worry or be embarrassed by her name," Ben predicted.

Ivy giggled in agreement. "You're probably right." She sobered and fixed him with an intense look. "You know, Ben, I asked you to come over here because I wanted to talk to you."

"Oh? About what?"

"I have a confession to make. I really miss having you in my life." She paused, picking her words carefully. "Having you with me when Rekia was born convinced me that I need your friendship."

"My friendship." Ben nodded his understanding. "I have been, and I will always be, your friend."

"I know," Ivy nodded," but lately you've been an absent friend. I don't want that, Ben. I want us to go back to spending time together."

"And what about Keith?" Ben had to ask. "What will he say about this?"

"Keith is Rekia's father, and that's all I've committed to. He can't pick my friends, and he can't run my life." Ivy put her hand on his shoulder. "I know it's a little selfish of me, and I'll understand if you don't want this, but I really do miss you, and I want my daughter to know you, too."

Ben sighed and surrendered, knowing he was entering a potentially dangerous emotional minefield. "Of course I want this. I will be for you and Rekia whatever you need me to be."

They fell into an easy rhythm, Ben and Ivy seeing each other once a week or so, usually for a movie or an outing in the park or the mall with the baby. They worked out together, Ben encouraging Ivy, who was determined to lose the extra weight she'd gained during the pregnancy.

Keith worked very hard to fill up the other spaces in her life. He became a regular fixture at her apartment, and even Ivy had to admit he was wonderful with the baby. She felt her heart softening toward Keith as she watched him cuddle and care for his daughter. Keith pressed her for a commitment, but Ivy deferred, saying she was too busy learning how to be a mother to worry about anything else.

All in all, it was a very happy time for Ivy. She had the friendship and support of a man she respected greatly, and the father of her baby was stepping up to his role more enthusiastically than she ever imagined he would.

Ivy tried to convince herself she was content and fulfilled, but there was an emptiness that lingered around the edges of her happiness. She couldn't identify it, but when she was honest with herself, she knew it was there.

One beautiful sunny day in late May, when Rekia was two-and-a-half months old, Ivy and Ben took the baby out for a walk. They headed to a park in Ivy's neighborhood that had a small duck pond. Rekia always squealed with delight when the ducks quacked and strutted around the pond.

Once they reached the park, they found a bench near the pond. Ben and Ivy sat down, with Rekia bouncing on Ben's knee watching the ducks.

"You seem a little quiet today," Ben observed. "Anything wrong?"

Ivy shook her head. "Not wrong, exactly. Just not right."

"Come again?"

"I feel like something's missing. Like there is something I need that I can't quite reach."

"Something like what?" Ben studied her closely.

"I just don't know," she said, frustrated. "But whatever it is, I have a feeling I need it to make my life complete."

Ben gave a low whistle. "Wow, that's some heavy-duty something. Can I help?"

Ivy shook her head. "I'm just in a mood today. Forget I said anything. It's a beautiful day—let's just enjoy it."

"Whatever you say." Ben turned his attention to the gurgling baby on his lap. "What do you think about that, Rekia? Are you enjoying the day?" A cooing giggle was his response. Ben stood and carried the baby closer to the water's edge. Ivy watched as he pointed out the ducks for her.

Why isn't this enough? Ivy wondered. *Why am I not satisfied with having a beautiful baby and wonderful friends who support me?* Frustration mounting at her inability to find an answer, Ivy stood and prepared the stroller to leave.

"Ben," she called, "can we head back now?"

"But we just got here," he started to complain, but the look on her face stopped him cold. "Uh, sure, Ivy. No problem." He put Rekia in the stroller and stood back as Ivy fastened the safety harnesses.

During the walk home, Ivy was quiet and moody. Ben wondered at her shift in mood, but decided not to press her. When they reached her apartment, she held the door open for him to enter. Ben gave her a questioning look.

"I need you to help me get the stroller upstairs. I'll take the baby, and if you would, you bring the stroller."

Ben nodded. She gently unfastened the baby and lifted her out of the stroller. Rekia had fallen asleep during the walk home, so Ivy mounted the stairs very slowly so as not to wake her. At the apartment, Ivy left the door open for Ben and headed back to the bedroom to put Rekia in her crib. She was tucking the baby in when Ben appeared in the doorway to the bedroom.

"Can I kiss her good night?" he asked.

"Of course." Ivy stepped to the side of the crib to make room.

Ben bent over the railing and brushed a tender kiss on Rekia's head. "Sleep tight, angel. Pleasant dreams."

Ivy motioned for him to follow her out of the nursery. After grabbing the handset of the baby monitor, she closed the door.

"There's no way she's out for the night," Ivy said," but she ought to sleep for a good long while. The fresh air did her good."

When they reached the living room, Ivy gestured toward the sofa. "Have a seat. Can I get you something to drink?"

Ben hesitated. "Are you sure you wouldn't rather

be alone? You seem to have a lot on your mind today."

"Don't be silly, Ben. Have a seat and let me get you a cold drink. That's the least I can do before you go." When he still didn't move, she added, "I'm fine . . . really."

"OK," Ben sounded skeptical. He settled on the sofa and reached for the remote control. "Is it all right if I turn the TV on? The basketball play-offs are on now."

"Sure," Ivy said as she walked to the kitchen. "Just keep it down low so it doesn't wake the baby."

Ben nodded his understanding and switched to the game. In the kitchen, Ivy rummaged around for something to offer her guest. She was astounded to realize she only had bottles of expressed breast milk, baby juice, water, and milk. She slammed the refrigerator door. Suddenly she felt overcome with emotion. She braced the countertop with her hands and took deep breaths of air, trying to fight back irrational tears.

Ben had heard the commotion from the kitchen and came to see what was wrong. When he saw her hunched over the counter, struggling for control, he went to her and put his hand on her shoulder.

"Ivy? What is it?"

The sound of his concerned voice and the gentle touch of his hand shattered her thin veneer of control, and she began to sob.

"I don't have anything adult to offer you to

drink," she managed between sobs. "All I have is baby stuff and water."

Ben was thoroughly confused. "It's OK, Ivy. I wasn't thirsty. Don't worry about it."

Ivy shook her head. "You don't understand. All I am now is a mother. Everything I have and everything I do is focused on that one job—being Rekia's mother. I've forgotten how to be Ivy—I've forgotten how to be a woman."

Ben gently turned her around to face him and gathered her into his arms. "That's not true," he crooned as he stroked her hair. "You are a beautiful, vibrant woman. Motherhood has only enhanced that."

Ivy rested her head against the solid wall of his chest, reveling in the feel of his arms around her, until the tears began to subside.

Ben pulled back slightly and rubbed his thumb across her cheek, wiping away her tears. "Better now?" he whispered.

Ivy looked up into his soulful eyes and suddenly realized what she had been missing. She lifted her hand and wound it around the back of his neck, gently guiding his lips down to meet hers.

The kiss was electric. Suddenly all the pent-up need and longing they each felt was released in a sensual torrent. Their tongues mingled and tasted, laved and suckled until they were both breathless. Ben cupped her bottom and pulled her hard against his body. She pressed against him and felt his erection growing against her belly.

Still locked in the kiss, he bent slightly and lifted her from the floor. She wrapped her legs around his waist and her arms around his neck, trusting him to support her. He backed out of the kitchen and laid her on the nearby dinette table. He pulled away from her lips to sear steamy kisses along her neck and collarbone. Ivy's head dropped back and a low moan escaped from her lips. Ben's hands were everywhere on her body, touching, caressing, arousing. When his hands found her breasts, Ivy's back arched. His lips claimed hers again and they shared deeply passionate kisses until that wasn't enough for either of them. Ben pulled back to study her closely.

"Ivy, if you're going to stop me, stop me now." His voice was a low rumble in his chest.

Ivy shook her head and reached for the hem of his T-shirt. She pulled it up and over his head. "I don't want you to stop," she answered. "I need you to make love to me—now."

Ben needed no further encouragement. Their clothes were quickly discarded in piles around the table. Ivy slid off the table and pulled him down to the floor. They lay side by side on the soft carpeting, kissing, touching, rediscovering. She rolled Ben onto his back and took his shaft into her hands. With smooth fluid motions, she caressed him, driving Ben right to the edge.

"Do you have any protection?" she whispered.

Ben nodded, not trusting his voice enough to speak, and reached for his pants. After a moment, he presented a foil packet he'd fished out of his wallet.

"You really are quite the boy scout," she teased. "Always prepared." She took the packet and tore open the package. With passionate deliberation, she eased the condom on. Ben started to rise, but Ivy pushed him back. She leaned over and kissed him, then swung her leg over his body, straddling him. Ben's entire body felt the charge as she guided his shaft inside of her. For one long intense moment, neither of them moved. Instead they were perfectly still, experiencing the shock waves that emanated from their connection.

Then Ben pushed himself up into a sitting position, supporting his weight and Ivy's on his elbows. Ivy began to move, slowly at first, but then as her need for release mounted, with more speed. Ben matched her tempo and pace, and they moved together in an erotic ballet. Ivy reached the pinnacle first. A shudder coursed through her body, beginning at her core and radiating until her every cell screamed with release. Spent, she collapsed against Ben's chest.

Ben held her to him and shifted so that she lay under him. Still supported on his elbows, Ben drove into her with hard, insistent thrusts. Ivy wrapped her legs around his hips, urging him on, giving him easier access. Ben's thrusts increased until suddenly he tensed. He had to bite down on his bottom lip to keep from crying out as his seed rushed from his body. He relaxed his body and lay against Ivy, claiming her lips once again.

After a moment, he moved away from Ivy and lay on his side facing her. It was then that he noticed her tears.

"Ivy! Are you OK? Did I hurt you?" Fear and concern colored his eyes.

"No," she said, wiping her eyes. "I have never felt better in my life. You don't know how badly I needed that." She shook her head. "I didn't know how badly I needed that."

"But you're crying."

"I'm just overcome with emotion. I can't explain it. But I'm not hurt, Ben. I promise."

He took her into his arms and held her against his chest. She rested her head on him.

"I don't know what happens now," she said softly. "I don't know what this means for our relationship."

"Shhh," Ben whispered. "It doesn't have to mean anything. I am, and I continue to be, your friend."

Satisfied, Ivy snuggled closer to his chest and allowed herself to doze off.

Twenty

By the end of May, Keith decided it was time to set things right. *Rekia is almost three months old,* he thought. *It's time for her parents to make her legitimate. Besides, people at the bank are beginning to talk. It doesn't look good for an executive like me to be an unmarried father.* Keith began his campaign with a visit to Ivy's parents.

"Grace, Albert, thank you for seeing me."

"Keith, don't be silly, why wouldn't we see you? You're our granddaughter's father," Grace said.

"That's exactly what I wanted to talk to you about. I don't want to be just your granddaughter's father." He leaned forward in the chair he was sitting on. "I want to be your daughter's husband."

"Well, that's not exactly news," Albert said. "And why are you telling us?"

"Because I'd like your help. I've been trying to convince Ivy we should go on and get married, and she's considering it, but I think she's still embarrassed by what happened last year. I think she's concerned about how it will look." Keith put on his most pitiful expression. "I was hoping you could talk to her, get her to see it would be all right, that in fact it would be good for Rekia if her parents got married."

"Embarrassment? That's why you think Ivy won't marry you?" Albert was incredulous. "That is certainly not what she said to us."

"Albert!" Grace's head whirled to face him. "Let the boy speak." She turned back to Keith. "Do you think something has changed since last year?"

"Yes, ma'am, I do. I know Ivy said she didn't love me the way a wife should love a husband, but that was almost a year ago. A lot has changed since then, mainly, now we have a child together. Our feelings have grown, and we've grown closer because of Rekia." Keith reached for Grace's hand. "Grace, I do not want my daughter to grow up with the stigma of unmarried parents. I want her to have my last name, and come home from school to a house with two loving parents. Please, won't you talk to Ivy?"

Grace nodded immediately. "Of course I will." She ignored Albert's derisive snort.

Keith's next stop was Ben's house. It took him some investigating, but he eventually found Ben's home address and phone number. It was out of sheer curiosity that Ben allowed Keith to come over when he called.

"Thank you for seeing me," Keith inserted the proper amount of humility in his voice. "You didn't have to."

"I know that, but I have to admit, I'm curious." Ben gestured for Keith to come in to the apartment. "What on earth could you have to say to me?"

"It's about Ivy."

"I figured that."

"It's about me and Ivy," Keith amended. "I've asked Ivy to marry me again, and she's considering it, but part of what is holding her back is you."

"Me?" Ben's brow furrowed. "How am I holding her back?"

"You are confusing her. She can't sort out her feelings with you around. I've come to ask you to step off."

"Ivy and I are just friends," Ben said defensively.

"You may be friends," Keith agreed," but you aren't *just* friends. There's something else going on between you. I know it, you know it, and Ivy knows it."

"Man, even if what you say is true, why on earth would I step off to make room for you?"

"Truthfully, it's not for me, it's for Rekia." Keith studied Ben intently. "Rekia deserves to have an intact family, and I'm asking you not to interfere with that. It's real simple. If you back away and give Ivy a chance to think clearly, she will see that marrying me is the best thing for our daughter."

Ben felt a small burning sensation in his chest—nothing alarming, just enough of a feeling to let him know a heartbreak was coming up fast. Suddenly he could no longer hear Keith's words. Instead the advice his mother and sister had given him months ago filled his head: *This Ivy will reconcile with her baby's father, and even though I don't think it will last, that doesn't mean I think you ought to be around, waiting to pick up the pieces. There's nothing in it for you Ben. Nothing but heartache and pain.* He could hear his mother's voice as clearly as if she stood next to him. *I'll bet you dollars to donuts that Ivy and her baby's daddy will be back together before the baby turns a year old. And you'll be standing around with your heart in your hands if you don't walk away now. You need to get while the getting's good.* He shook his head, ruefully remembering Dionne's words. *Guess I missed my chance to "get,"* he thought.

"Well, Stephens? What do you say?" Keith's question brought Ben back to the present. "I wouldn't be here if it weren't for the baby. If it were any other circumstance, I'd say may the best man win. But I have to put my pride aside for the sake of my daughter."

Ben could find no words to say. His heart would not let him say what his mind and conscious dictated. He looked away from Keith and nodded.

Keith took the movement for the concession it was. "Thank you, Stephens. You'll see this is best for everybody." Keith quickly turned and let himself out.

Ben stood alone in his living room, his heart heavy. "Best for everybody . . ."

Although Ivy tried to deny it, something had changed between her and Ben since they'd made love. She could sense him pulling back from her, but she didn't know why. He didn't come around as much, and when she called him, he was almost always tied up with something else. Ivy slowly became convinced she'd jeopardized their friendship by making love to him.

A lot has changed between the first time we were together and now. Ben probably doesn't want the responsibility of a child. I have to respect that. She decided she wouldn't try to press Ben for more than he could give. *He said he'd always be my friend . . . I guess that'll have to be enough.*

But if Ben was backing away, Keith was applying a full-court press. He was unabashedly trying to woo her and persuade her to marry him. He came by regularly, spending time with both Ivy and Rekia. Ivy watched as he doted on his daughter. Her heart swelled as Keith and Rekia bonded, so much so that Rekia's whole face brightened up when Keith came into the room.

Grace was doing her part. She spoke with Ivy on several occasions, each time singing the praises of marriage to Keith. Ivy felt herself weakening under the onslaught.

One day, as she watched Keith give Rekia her bottle, she suddenly couldn't remember why not marrying Keith seemed so important.

"Keith, do you still want to get married?"

Keith looked up, surprised. "You know I do."

"Well, I've been thinking. Maybe we should."

A look of triumph spread across Keith's face. He quickly sat the baby in her swing and rushed over to hug Ivy.

"It's about time!" He swept her into his arms. "We'll be so happy together, the three of us—you'll see!" He bent to kiss her. Ivy yielded to the kiss, but a part of her held back, as if watching the scene from a distance.

Ivy realized that she felt nothing when Keith kissed her, and despite her best intentions, she couldn't help comparing his kisses to Ben's. When Keith released her, she looked up at him, willing herself to feel passionate about him. "The three of us," she repeated, "we will be happy, won't we?"

"Yes." Keith was confident. "Yes, we will. Now you just leave everything to me. I'll take care of getting the wedding together. I want us to get married on the same day that we should have gotten married on all along."

"June thirteenth? Keith, that's barely two weeks away!"

"Don't you worry about a thing. I'll handle it!" He headed toward the door, rushing to take care of the arrangements. He turned back to face her. "You still have that dress from before, right?"

Ivy hesitated, remembering her flight to the El train, the mayhem that ensued, the destruction of the dress, and meeting Ben. A small smile played about her lips. "Uh, no. I don't still have that dress."

"Well, never mind. We'll find something appropriate for you to wear." He opened the door and headed out. "I'll talk to you later," he called as he bounded down the stairs.

Ivy closed the door behind him and found herself alone with her thoughts. *This is the right thing to do, isn't it?* she mused. Just then, Rekia cried because her swing had stopped. As Ivy went to restart the swing, she tried to convince herself that everything would work out fine. *Rekia deserves the best of everything,* she thought. *I'd do anything to ensure she has a good life.*

The swing started again, the baby gurgled happily, and Ivy tried to block out the uncertainty that nagged at her soul.

Twenty-one

"I wanted you to hear it from me first. Ivy has finally agreed to marry me."

"Congratulations," she said dryly. "I'm sure you'll be very happy together."

"I don't think you mean that, but no matter." Keith lifted his chin confidently. "Ivy and our daughter and I will be very happy."

The woman snorted. "So why are you telling me? What does this have to do with me?"

Keith squared his shoulders. "Since Ivy and I will be getting married, I can't be with you anymore. It wouldn't be right."

"Oh, and it's been right up until now?"

"It hasn't been wrong," Keith hedged. "But it would be wrong to continue. It was fun while it lasted, but all good things must come to an end."

"Just like that? You think you can just waltz in here and break up with me after all this time and it'll be over because you say it's over?" The woman shook her head in amazement. "What a colossal ego you have."

"Whatever." Keith turned to leave. "I just wanted to be up front with you. Oh, and Ivy will probably ask you to be a bridesmaid again."

"What?"

"We're going to have the big wedding I was denied last year, so she'll probably want you to stand up with her again. I sincerely hope you don't disappoint my fiancée." Keith left then, closing the door behind him.

The woman stood in her apartment motionless and stunned. Slowly, anger began to eat away at her.

"How dare he! I will not be discarded like yesterday's paper." She stalked over to her phone and snatched the receiver off its hook. "I should tell Miss Ivy everything. Let's see how she reacts to that!" She punched in the first three digits of Ivy's phone number, then stopped. Slowly she replaced the receiver.

"No," she decided. "I'm not going to say anything. Let Ivy marry that snake. It's just a matter of time before he comes slithering back over here because she's not enough woman to keep him at home. No, I'll keep his dirty little secret, and then he'll be mine for good."

Ivy decided she needed to tell Ben about the wedding in person. She stopped by his apartment one day, unannounced.

"Ivy! I wasn't expecting to see you today." Ben's face registered his surprise.

"No, and I'm sorry I didn't call first, but I knew if I did, you'd have some reason why you couldn't see me, and I needed to talk to you today." Ivy cocked her head at him. "May I come in?"

"Of course. I'm sorry." Ben stepped aside for her to enter. "Where's Rekia?"

"She's with my parents today. I wanted to talk to you without any distractions."

"Well, you're here. Talk." Ben gestured toward the sofa.

Ivy sat down before she began. "I wanted you to know that I have agreed to marry Keith. Our wedding will be on June thirteenth."

"So he finally convinced you." Ben shrugged. "I wish you all the best."

Ivy studied him closely. "You don't seem surprised."

"Should I be? Keith has been trying to marry you since the day we met." Ben looked at her, and his resolve to back off began to fall away. "Just tell me one thing," he said. "Do you love him?"

"He's Rekia's father."

"There's no doubt about that, but that was not my question. I asked you if you loved him."

"Keith has always been very special to me. Rekia adores him and he adores her. We'll have a good life," she finished defensively.

"You are not answering my question," he pointed out.

"What do you want me to say?" Ivy was getting angry. "You want me to declare my undying love for Keith? Neither of us would believe that. But I love my daughter, and I want her to have the kind of family I had growing up."

Ben shook his head sadly. "Ivy, when we met that day on the El train, you running for your very life, with your dress in shreds, you said to me—and I've

never forgotten it—you said not marrying Keith
was absolutely the right decision, but you made it
the wrong way. You had no regrets about not marrying him; you were just sorry you had caused such
a scene. That was less than a year ago. Have your
feelings changed that much since then?"

"A lot of things have changed since then," she
said quietly. "I have to do what's best for my
daughter."

Ben wanted to shake her until she could see the
mistake she was making. "It's like you're sacrificing
yourself on the altar of family," he said angrily.
"Ivy, you told me once, and I quote, The road to
hell is paved with good intentions. Why can't you
see that's exactly what you're doing?"

Ivy jumped up from the sofa. "Stop throwing my
words in my face," she yelled. "I have to do the
right thing . . . marrying Keith is the right thing."

"If I had known you didn't really love him, I
would have never agreed to back off." Ben's sad
words were spoken more to himself than to her.

"What did you say?" she demanded.

"Nothing," he shook his head. "Go get married
and be happy."

"You did say something," she insisted. "Tell me
what!"

Ben debated for a moment, then, "To hell with
it," he muttered. "You really want to know? OK,
your fiancé came by here a few weeks ago and
asked me to back off. He said I was clouding your
judgment, and without me in the picture, you
would be able to recognize how very much you
loved him, and how very happy you two could be

together. I agreed, against my better judgment, because I thought your so-called family deserved a chance to develop." Ben shook his head. "But I see clearly now that you do not love Keith. You are marrying him because you think that's what you're supposed to do. Ivy, you saved yourself from that mistake once; don't turn around and make it again."

Ivy stumbled back, reeling from his words. "Keith came here to talk to you? I didn't know . . ." She spun on her heels and practically ran for the door. As she headed out of the apartment, Ben called after her.

"Do what's right for yourself, Ivy. Make the choice that's right for you and to hell with anybody else."

Alone with her thoughts, Ivy tried to process what Ben had told her. *So that's why he backed away . . . not because he couldn't handle being with my child but because Keith laid a guilt trip on him. I wonder if things would have turned out differently if Keith hadn't made that visit.*

Ivy shook her head, clearing away the unsettling thoughts. Keeping her mind deliberately blank, Ivy started her car and headed to her parents' home, needing to hold her daughter, needing confirmation of her choice.

"OK, the church is confirmed, and even though the florist complained that he would have to work overtime, the flowers will be there." Keith sat at her dinette table ticking off items on his checklist. "I'm picking up the invitations at the printers tomorrow, but I'll probably have to have them hand delivered, since time is so short."

Ivy laughed and shook her head. "You're like some kind of crazed wedding machine," she said. "How are you going to get everything together so quickly?"

Keith looked up from his list. "Just watch me."

"You know, it would be a lot easier to go to city hall and find a justice of the peace," she suggested.

"No way!" He slammed his hand down on the clipboard. "I want the same big wedding we should have had. I don't think you fully realize how embarrassed I was last year. I want a chance to redeem myself in front of all those people." He looked intensely at her. "You owe me that."

Ivy said nothing; instead she backed away from the table and went to see to Rekia. *I'm doing the right thing*, she told herself as she held her daughter close to her heart. *I am doing the right thing . . .*

The days passed in a whirlwind of activity. Keith was in the center of the storm, orchestrating the wedding plan with all the finesse of a battle general. Ivy didn't allow herself to think; she just went along with the plans. The one detail Keith had left up to her was the choice of a dress, but she found that she was dragging her feet on even that. Her mother finally showed up one day, two days before the wedding, with a large garment bag.

"Keith thought you might need a little help picking a dress," Grace said. "So I got this one for you. I hope you like it."

"I'm sure it's fine, Mom." Ivy didn't even look at the dress. "I trust your judgment."

"Do you, Ivy? Do you really? Because I want you to know I am confident this marriage is the absolute best thing for you and Ricki."

"Rekia, Mother!" Ivy spun to face her. "My daughter's name is Rekia. Why can't you say that?"

"It's just not a very common name, that's all. It takes a little getting used to." Grace studied her carefully. "What's wrong with you?"

"Nothing. Everything's fine. Thanks for the dress." Ivy crossed the room to hold open the door.

Grace took the hint. "It's all going to be all right, Ivy. Honestly." Grace swung her purse over her shoulder and left the apartment.

Ivy closed the door behind her mother and turned to stare at the garment bag lying on the sofa.

Why am I doing this? She asked herself at last. *Because I don't want to embarrass anybody? Mother can't even say my daughter's name. Is protecting her from embarrassment my responsibility?* She walked over to a chair and sank down into it. *Because Rekia deserves a family? What is a family, anyway? And what about what I deserve? When do I get to focus on myself?* Ivy's shoulders slumped as she struggled to find the answers she needed for her future.

Twenty-two

"OK, listen," Keith instructed over the phone. "The limousine will be there to pick you up at eleven A.M. Rekia is with your parents; they'll bring her to the church. Your dress will already be there. All you need to do is get in the car and come get married."

"Listen Keith, we need to talk," Ivy began.

"We'll talk at the reception," Keith interrupted, "and for the rest of our lives. I've got to go now. There are a couple of final details I need to tend to before the wedding. I'll see you at the church." He hung up before she could say another word.

Ivy replaced the phone slowly. She checked her watch; she had an hour before the limo arrived. She went to her bathroom to get ready—ready for what, she wasn't exactly sure.

You still don't love him. The small voice of her soul she had been studiously ignoring for the last two weeks finally made itself heard. *You don't love Keith like a wife should, and you know it.*

Ivy scrubbed her face roughly, trying to quiet the voice, but it would no longer be still.

Yes, he's a good father, and yes he's a decent guy, but you don't love him. His kisses leave you cold. She forced herself to meet her eyes in the mirror. *But can I do that again? Do I dare leave Keith at the altar a second time?*

This isn't about Keith. The war for her soul continued. *This is about you, what you want, what you need, what you feel.* And then she allowed herself to say the name she had been avoiding for weeks.

"Ben . . ."

You know love, the now loud voice continued, *and you know where it is, and it's not at that church.*

The buzz of her door intercom broke into her thoughts. She hurried through the apartment to answer the buzzer.

"Limo's here, ma'am," a male voice said.

"I'll be right down." Ivy grabbed her purse and headed out the door. She suddenly felt lighter than she had in weeks. As she climbed into the limo, she gave the driver an alternate address.

"But I'm supposed to take you right to the church," the driver protested.

"It'll be OK," she assured him. "We'll be going there next."

Mumbling under his breath, the limo driver changed directions to follow Ivy's orders.

"Wait here a minute," Ivy said when they had arrived. "I'll be right back." She bounded from the limo and all but ran up to Ben's apartment. She rang the bell and waited impatiently for him to answer.

I know love, she repeated in her mind, *and I know where it is.*

Several long moments passed with no answer at Ben's door. She rang again, and followed up with an insistent knocking. There was still no answer. Her heart fell as she scanned the street for his car and realized it wasn't there.

"Not home," she mumbled dejectedly. She turned to go back to the limo. "OK, take me to the church," she instructed the driver.

I will just talk to Ben later, she decided. *I will explain my feelings to him and hope and pray he feels the same. But whatever happens with Ben, I know I cannot marry Keith. And this time, I have to tell him face-to-face.*

When the limo stopped in front of the church, Ivy felt she was ready for what she had to do. The wedding was still more than an hour away, so the guests had not yet begun to arrive. She mounted the steps, confident that she was doing the right thing. Entering the church through a side door, she immediately went in search of Keith. She heard his voice coming from one of the Sunday school classrooms and headed in that direction.

"Thank you for not telling her," he was saying. "I knew that you would do the right thing. There's just no good reason for Ivy to know about us."

"I always try to do the right thing for you, Keith."

Ivy recognized the voice immediately. *Cherise?*

"And always remember that I'm here for you. When this ridiculous marriage of yours gets to be too much, Cherise will be nearby to tend to your needs. Just like I was the day that baby was born."

Ivy's eyes widened in shock. *Keith and Cherise? How long?* Then suddenly she realized that Keith's infidelity meant nothing to her. It was the final confirmation she needed to know that she did not love Keith enough to marry him.

She entered the classroom doorway and cleared her throat to make her presence known. Keith and Cherise jumped apart, guilty expressions on both of their faces.

"Keith, I have something to tell you, but maybe it won't be as hard for you to accept as I thought." Ivy raked over him with a disdainful look. "I can't marry you. I'm sorry we're going through this again, but I just can't marry you. In the long run it would be bad for everybody, especially me."

"Why?" The single syllable exploded from Keith with the force of an atom bomb. "Why can't you marry me? Because of her?" He gestured dismissively at Cherise. "She means nothing—she was an itch, and now she's been scratched." He ignored Cherise's gasp of indignation. "Don't let this meaningless liaison ruin our future."

Cherise stood with her hands on her hips, glaring daggers at him. "An itch?" she screeched. "How dare you!"

He held up his hand in her direction. "Hush! This is not about you."

"That's right," Ivy interrupted. "It's not about her. It's not about you. It's about me. I can't spend the rest of my life pretending to feel something I don't. Not for you, not for Mom, and not even for Rekia. I don't love you, Keith. And just so you'll know, I made this decision long before I learned about your *meaningless liaison*."

"So what are you saying?" Keith sneered. "You

gonna hit the road like the last time and leave me to clean up your mess?"

Ivy shook her head. "No, I'll handle the guests. As a matter of fact, if you'd like, the limo is right outside. If you leave now, you can get away before most of them arrive." Her face softened. "I'm not trying to embarrass or humiliate you, Keith," she looked at Cherise, "although you didn't seem to be trying to spare me a similar fate. I just know what I know, and I know I can't marry you. It's as simple as that."

"It's him, isn't it?" Keith demanded. "Stephens is the reason you won't marry me, isn't he?"

Ivy shook her head. "I haven't spoken to Ben," she said truthfully. She stopped short of confessing her love for Ben. There seemed to be no reason to hurt Keith like that. "If you're going to take the limo, you should probably go now," she said. "People are starting to arrive."

"What about my daughter?" Keith demanded. "You aren't going to try and keep her from me, are you?"

"Never." Ivy raised her hand. "I swear to you. I know how much you love her. I would never interfere with that."

Keith nodded. "You've made up your mind, haven't you?"

"Yes. I have." Ivy was definite.

"You've made a mistake—again," Keith shot back. "But I'll respect your decision. Only this time, don't expect me to chase after you. When I leave this church, I'm gone for good. The only time you'll see me is when I come to get Rekia."

Ivy nodded. "I understand. And I'm sorry if I've hurt you again."

Keith made a face and then ducked out of the room, hurrying to the side door and the waiting limousine.

Ivy slowly turned to face Cherise. "I thought you were my friend."

"I was . . . I am your friend."

Ivy snorted. "With friends like you . . ." Ivy's voice trailed off, leaving the sentence unfinished. "There's just one thing I want to know. Was Keith with you the night Rekia was born?"

Cherise shrugged. "He was feeling stressed and overwhelmed. He just needed to get away from the pressure for a night."

"He needed to get away from the pressure?" Ivy unexpectedly laughed. "I was struggling to produce a life, and *he* needed to get away from the pressure?"

"Ivy, I . . . ," Cherise began.

"You know what," Ivy cut her off, "you should probably leave, too. There's not really anything else for us to say to one another, is there Miss—what did he call you—Itch?"

Cherise flinched and looked away from Ivy's penetrating stare. She spun on her heel and ducked out the same door Keith had just used.

Keith and Cherise. Ivy shook her head. *Damn, was I a fool, or what?* Still, she didn't feel any anger, just a sort of bewilderment at her own naivete.

She squared her shoulders and put the incident out of her mind. She had a few more people to face. She went into the dressing room where her friends were getting ready.

"Ivy! You're late," Danielle rushed over to her. "We were starting to get worried."

"I'm fine," Ivy said. "Listen, guys, there's something I need to tell you."

"I knew it!" Kim suddenly burst into laughter. "Pay up, girls! I told you she wouldn't marry him."

"You what?" Ivy couldn't help but laugh. "You bet on whether or not I'd get married?"

"Yep, and thank you for making me some money today," Kim said.

"Ivy, are you sure?" Trina looked concerned. "And I'm not just asking so I won't have to pay Miss Know-it-all over there."

Ivy nodded. "I have never been more sure of anything in my life. I don't love Keith. I tried to convince myself I did, but I don't and I deserve better than a loveless marriage." She decided not to say anything about Keith and Cherise.

That will come out soon enough, she thought, *and it really doesn't have anything to do with my decision.*

"So what now?" Danielle asked.

"Now, I've got to go tell a church full of people that there is not going to be a wedding today," Ivy said. "And then I've got to go and claim my life."

"What does that mean?" Trina looked confused.

"I think I know," Kim said smugly. "It's Ben, isn't it? You have fallen in love with Ben."

Ivy shrugged. "I don't know how he feels, and I don't know what's going to happen, but I know that I could not possibly marry Keith feeling the way I do about Ben."

"Then you shouldn't," Danielle agreed. "Even though it cost me twenty-five dollars."

Ivy laughed. "It's on me."

Ivy left the dressing room to go into the sanctuary. A hush fell over the full room when she appeared, dressed in jeans and a T-shirt. She walked to the front and reached for the microphone.

"Um, ladies and gentlemen, may I have your attention." She cleared her throat. "First of all, I want to thank you all for making time in your schedules on such short notice to come here today. Unfortunately, I have some bad news. Keith has decided not to marry me after all." She hoped the gentle lie would help Keith salvage some dignity in the days to come. "I apologize for any inconvenience and I hope we can count on your friendship and support in the future." She put the microphone back on its stand and headed out of the sanctuary, ignoring both the gasps of surprise and the knowing nods.

She met her parents in the hall outside the sanctuary; Grace was carrying Rekia in her arms.

"Ivy, what did you just say?" Her mother looked scandalized.

"I think you heard me, Mom."

Grace's eyes immediately filled with tears. "Oh, Ivy, not again," she wailed. She held out the baby to Ivy. "This beautiful little girl deserves an intact family—a mommy and a daddy. How can you deprive her of that?"

Ivy gently lifted Rekia from her mother's arms. Cuddling the baby close to her chest, Ivy turned a pleading look to her mother. "Please try not to judge me too harshly. I just couldn't do it . . . I tried to convince myself I could, but I couldn't because I don't love Keith. I hope you can come to understand that."

Grace shook her head vehemently. "You have been given a chance to right a wrong—don't blow it again."

Slowly, Ivy's expression turned from pleading to resolute. "You're right, Mom. I have been given a chance to right a wrong—or in this case, stop a wrong before it even happens. I deserve more than a loveless marriage, and Rekia deserves more than parents who are together out of a misguided sense of obligation or duty."

"But Ivy, Keith is such a wonderful catch—"

"That's debatable," Ivy mumbled. "But this isn't about Keith, Mother. This is about me. I don't love him. I can't say it any plainer than that." She shifted Rekia so that the baby rested on her hip. "The first time I held my daughter, I knew what true, unconditional love was. For a long time, I thought that love would be enough for me, that I could love Rekia enough to make up for the fact that I didn't love Keith. But I was wrong."

"I just want you to be happy," Grace whispered.

Ivy nodded. "Mom, I know now that love is not an illusion. I know love, and I know where it is. If you truly want me to be happy, you will support me and trust my judgment.''

"But Keith—" Grace began.

"Stop it, Grace." Albert stepped between his wife and daughter. "We're talking about Ivy's life here . . . let her live it her way."

Grace's look traveled from Albert to Ivy; then she lowered her head and surrendered to the tears that had threatened since the conversation began. Albert wrapped strong arms around her, supporting her as she cried. "It's going to be OK, baby," Albert soothed. "Ivy is doing the right thing for her."

Grace nodded against his chest. "I know," she conceded finally. She eased out of his arms and turned to face Ivy. "I understand unconditional love, too," she said. She opened her arms and gathered her daughter and granddaughter close to her heart. "You are a strong, beautiful woman, Ivy. I trust your judgment."

Albert nodded his approval. "You know we'll support you whatever you do."

"I know, Daddy." Ivy returned Grace's hug. "I know."

She released her mother and faced her parents. "Can you guys watch Rekia for a few days? There is something I have to take care of."

Grace nodded and held out her arms to accept the baby. "Rekia will be fine. Go, follow your heart, find Ben."

As Ivy passed the baby, she looked at Grace, wonder in her eyes. "How did you know?"

"Please." Grace wiped at her tears. "I know my child."

Ivy hugged and kissed her mother; then she turned and ran out of the church. *I don't know where he is,* she thought, *but I will find him and I will talk to him, today.*

She started in the direction of the El station where she'd made her earlier escape. She had only taken a few steps when she saw him emerge from his car. Her heart flipped over in her chest at the sight of him.

Ben . . . she breathed the name as if the essence of life could be found in that one syllable.

He approached her slowly. "Church is that way," he said, nodding in the opposite direction.

"I know," she said. "I wasn't going to the church."

"Oh?" A heartful of questions hung in the word.

"What are you doing here?" she asked, holding her breath as she waited for his answer.

Ben hesitated for a moment. "I came to see you," he said finally. "I couldn't believe you were going to marry someone else, so I had to see for myself." He took another step in her direction. "Ivy, I love you. I know this is a really bad time to be telling you this, but—"

She reached out and placed her fingertips against his lips. "No, let me. I'm not marrying Keith. Not today, not ever. I don't love him. And I'm not going to sacrifice my happiness on the altar of family."

He smiled against her fingers as he recognized the words he'd said to her days earlier. The smile faded a bit. He moved her fingers aside. "What about Rekia? Keith is still her father."

"I'm not trying to deny Keith's right to be Rekia's father. That is who he is . . . nothing I could or would do can ever change that. But the truth I hadn't seen, at least until now, is that Keith being Rekia's father does not automatically mean that Keith has to be my husband." She looked into Ben's eyes, willing him to understand. "We can make our family whatever we want it to be. Families come in all kinds of constructions. I believe it is much more important for my daughter to be raised by people who love her and who are happy with their lives. I understand now that if I married Keith just for Rekia's sake, nobody would be happy for very long. It took me a long time, but I finally understand that Rekia's happiness and well-being does not have to come at the cost of mine."

She opened her heart and said the words that had burned in her soul for longer than seemed possible. "Ben, I love you, too."

Ben smiled then, a rich, full smile that radiated from his face until his entire body seemed suffused by its glow. He pulled her into his arms and they kissed—a kiss that carried the promise of a lifetime of better days ahead.

ABOUT THE AUTHOR

Crystal Wilson Harris is an Associate Professor of Developmental English at Sinclair Community College in her hometown of Dayton, Ohio. She holds a Bachelor's degree from Howard University in Washington, DC and a Master's degree from the University of Dayton.

Crystal enjoys spending time with her family and volunteering in various community service organizations. Her other interests include jazz, cyberspace, auto racing (watching, not driving—yet), a not-so-secret affinity for all things *Star Trek* (*Next Generation* only please), and an almost obsessive love for home improvement/decorating programs.

GOOD INTENTIONS is Crystal's fifth novel. Despite a schedule that has her juggling a full-time job, two kids, a dog, and a cat, she is currently hard at work on her next book. Crystal loves to hear from fans. Contact her via E-mail at CrystalWH@thekeyboard.com or snail mail at: P.O. Box 3643, Dayton, Ohio 45401-3643.

COMING IN FEBRUARY 2001
FROM ARABESQUE ROMANCES

__A REASON TO LOVE
by Marcia King-Gamble   1-58314-133-2   **$5.99**US/**$7.99**CAN
Niki Hamilton is burned-out. So when her friend invites her to vacation at the beach, Niki jumps at the chance. But when an emergency leaves her in charge of her pal's dating service, Niki suddenly meets the sexiest single dad she's ever laid eyes on.

__INFATUATION
by Sonia Icilyn   1-58314-217-7   **$5.99**US/**$7.99**CAN
Daytime star Desney Westbourne is determined to reclaim her reputation after a magazine article falsely smears her name. But she never expects the 24-7 coverage that editor Wade Beresford insists on to set the record straight, will spark a dangerously sensual attraction. . . .

__LOVE AFFAIR
by Bettye Griffin   1-58314-138-3   **$5.99**US/**$7.99**CAN
Austin Hughes has to get a wife. He needs a colleague to pose as his bride while he travels on business to West Africa. Desireé Mack is perfect for the job. But the chemistry that develops between them soon has Austin thinking she might be the perfect woman, period.

__LOVE NOTES
by Leslie Esdaile   1-58314-185-5   **$5.99**US/**$7.99**CAN
Nina Carpenter knows her marriage is in trouble—suddenly the differences that seemed so exciting when they met are now driving them apart. Then Tony's Jazz club is robbed, and Nina must choose between a solitary life—or fighting for the man she loves. . . .

Call toll free **1-888-345-BOOK** to order by phone or use this coupon to order by mail. *ALL BOOKS AVAILABLE FEBRUARY 1, 2001.*

Name_____

Address _____

City_____ State _____ Zip _____

Please send me the books I have checked above.

I am enclosing $_____

Plus postage and handling* $_____

Sales tax (in NY, TN, and DC) $_____

Total amount enclosed $_____

*Add $2.50 for the first book and $.50 for each additional book.
Send check or money order (no cash or CODs) to: **Kensington Publishing Corp., Dept. C.O., 850 Third Avenue, New York, NY 10022**
Prices and numbers subject to change without notice. Valid only in the U.S. All orders subject to availability. **NO ADVANCE ORDERS.**

Visit our website at **www.arabesquebooks.com.**